If I Was Your Girl

Also by Ni-Ni Simone

Shortie Like Mine

Published by Dafina Books

If I Was Your Girl

Ni-Ni Simone

Dafina Books for Young Readers
KENSINGTON PUBLISHING CORP.
http://www.kensingtonbooks.com

DAFINA BOOKS are published by

Kensington Publishing Corp.
850 Third Avenue
New York, NY 10022

All Kensington titles, imprints, and distributed lines are available at special quantity discounts for bulk purchases for sales promotion, premiums, fund-raising, educational, or institutional use.

Special book excerpts or customized printings can also be created to fit specific needs. For details, write or phone the office of the Kensington Special Sales Manager: Attn. Special Sales Department. Kensington Publishing Corp., 850 Third Avenue, New York, NY 10022. Phone: 1-800-221-2647.

Dafina and the Dafina logo Reg. U.S. Pat. & TM Off.

ISBN-13: 978-0-7582-2841-3
ISBN-10: 0-7582-2841-4

First Printing: October 2008
10 9 8 7 6 5 4 3 2 1

Printed in the United States of America

To my Taylor, who said,
"I can't believe Mommy would use the word
hollah.
She's not cool!"

To my Sydney,
whom I asked to perform her ballet routine,
and without warning,
she turned into Beyoncé,
dropped down,
and started sweeping the floor with it.
I'm just starting to recover.

And to my baby boy Zion,
whose favorite word is 'no.'

Acknowledgments

To my Savior and Lord Jesus Christ, if I had a thousand tongues, I couldn't thank you enough.

To my mother for helping me out when my deadlines were kicking my you know what!

To my father, who is simply honored that I named a character Melvin in my first book (LOL).

To my husband, Kevin, and my mother-in-law, Beulah, for all of your support.

To my editors and publishing families, thank you for believing in my talent, even when I have my days.

To Nakea Murray and Tiffany Colvin—it's official: 3 Chicks On Lit have entered the building.

To all of my family and friends, the gratitude and love I have for you could never be expressed in words. I thank you for being my biggest supporters. And to my author friends, where would I be if I couldn't call you and say, 'listen to this!' God Bless!

viii

To all of my fans, bookstores, book clubs, co-workers, my church family, message boards, and everyone else who has been with me during the course of my career, I want to thank you for everything. You mean the world!

And to all of the little girls who dream, I want you to dream big and know that as sure as this book is written, the sky is the limit!

Be sure to email me at *ninisimone@yahoo.com* or send me a friend request at myspace.com/nini_simone.

Hollah atcha gurl!
Peace

Drama Part 1

Play Your Position or Change Your Position

1

"This is my jam, right here!" I screamed as we drove down Bergen Street with the sounds of Playaz Circle's "Duffle Bag Boy" blasting from the car into the street. We'd just left the Hot 97 King of Rap concert at the Prudential Center and were still high from the night's festivities.

"Girl, did you see how Lil Wayne was looking at me?" my sister, Seven, said as she danced in the back seat.

"You lying, Seven," Tay laughed, as she drove down the street, looking at her in the rearview mirror. "You know Weezie was lookin' at me."

"I know y'all ain't on my baby daddy!" I stopped singing long enough to chime in.

"Girl, please," Seven snapped. "You got enough baby daddies!"

We all laughed as I turned up the volume and

started singing again. "*I ain't nevah ran from a damn thing and I damn sure ain't 'bout to pick today to start runnin'.*"

As I threw my arms in the air, Tay said, "Toi, ain't that Quamir's truck?" She pointed across Rector Street.

I looked at the tags on the black Escalade. "Hell, yeah." I turned the music down.

"And ain't that Shanice's house?" Seven asked. "I thought he stopped messing with her."

"We don't know if that's her house," I snapped defensively. "You always jumping to conclusions."

Tay looked at me out the corner of her eyes. "You need to stop frontin'," she spat, "you know that's where the skeezer lives." Tay double parked in the street, next to Quamir's truck. "Now the question is, what you gon' do about it?"

"Nothin'," Seven jumped in. "You don't bring it to nobody else's spot." She sucked her teeth. "If anything we can slice his tires and bounce."

"Slice his tires?" Tay snapped, "that is so whack." She looked at me. "You know this is ridiculous right? And I'm not slicing no tires or breaking no windows, he gon' put up or shut up. 'Cause frankly, I can't take you crying over this dude anymore."

"Confront him and what?" Seven spat. "If we not gon' key up his ride then we need to bounce." She turned to me. "You've seen it with your own eyes, so now you know you need to leave 'im alone." Seven wiggled her neck from side to side.

"Bounce?" Tay sucked her teeth. "Girl, please, we 'bout to handle this."

Neither of them had noticed that I hadn't said a word. I was in shock, but then again I wasn't. I just wasn't in the mood to react to something that obviously wasn't going to change, but there was no way I could let my sister or my best friend think I was gon' allow Quamir to keep playing me. I had to stand up for something, so I twisted my neck and rolled my eyes. "I'ma ring the trick's bell."

"There it is." Tay said, "there it is, and you know I got your back."

At least for pride's sake I had to pretend like I was strong. Strong enough, to at least beat this bitch's ass for being with my baby daddy. "I'm 'bout to wild-out!"

"This what you do," Tay said as we got out the car. "When she comes to the door, drag her ass down the stairs. Don't even show her no mercy. She knew Quamir was your dude, yet she keeps calling him over here. Nah, we gon' end this right now." Tay's lips popped twice as she zigzagged her neck. She was the spitting image of the ghetto twins in *ATL*, with the attitude to match, which is why I knew that if nothing else I could always count on her to be down with the get down. Even when I just wanted to curl up and die, she was on guard.

"You know this don't make no sense, right?"

Seven said as she got out the car. "Mommy will kick *our* asses if she knew we were out here like this! Forget Quamir!"

"Forget Quamir? Do you know how bad he keep doggin' this fool?" Tay pointed at me.

"Don't call me no fool." I rolled my eyes as we walked up the steps.

"My fault," she gave me a crooked smile. "You know what I mean. Anyway, Seven, do you know this is like . . . the nineteenth time we ready to pounce on ole boy? Girl, please forget Quamir. He's takin' time away from me and my man. I wish I would—"

"Tay." I was pissed and she was making it worse. "You don't even have a man."

"Exactly," she whispered as I rang the bell. "And I'm not gon' get one chasing behind yours."

"Excuse you?" I sucked my teeth.

"Don't get mad, kick ass. Show 'em what's really hood. I'm tired of this dude playing you every other week. Shit, I need some sleep."

"This don't make no sense." Seven tapped her foot standing behind me. I could feel the warmth of her breath as she sighed against my neck.

"For real, y'all," I said. "Not now, 'cause the way I feel, y'all 'bout to get it. So my suggestion to you," I looked at Seven and then at Tay, "is to fall back."

"Excuse you?" Seven blinked her eyes.

"Be clear," Tay spat. "T-skee ain't the one. Let Quamir and his new skeezer be the only ones you feel comfortable bringin' it to—"

"No, I don't appreciate—"

"Toi—" Tay interrupted me.

"Don't cut me off!"

"Would you shut up?" she said, tight-lipped with arched eyebrows. "Somebody's comin' to the door!"

Immediately, all the air left my body as I watched Quamir open the door with Shanice standing beside him. I couldn't believe this was happening to me, especially since I knew Shanice. I mean, we weren't friends, but we went to school together and she knew Quamir was my man.

I could feel my eyes knocking in the back of my head, but now was not the time to cry. So I held my tears back as best I could, and looked at Shanice's face. I couldn't deny how pretty she was, and for a moment I wondered if Quamir thought she was prettier than me. We were both the color of fresh apple butter, yet her eyes glistened like full moons, while mine were almond shaped. I had a dimpled smile and she had a wide one. Unless I had my hair flat ironed straight, it fell over my shoulders in an abundance of ocean waves, but ole girl wore a cheap blond clip weave. Wait a minute, I just found a flaw, at least my hair is real. Now I had the souped-up confidence I needed to handle my business. "This what you want, Quamir?"

"Yo'," he said, surprised. "What are you doing here?"

"What you think?" I pointed my hand like a gun in his face, yet looking dead in hers. "This the tramp you want?"

"What is she doin' at my door, Quamir? You don't be coming to my house!" Shanice screamed, jumping up and down, acting as if at any moment she was gon' bring it.

"I know she ain't stuntin'," Tay snapped. "Oh, hell no!"

"And what?" Shanice hunched her shoulders. "He don't want her and she knows it!"

True story, I wanted to just walk away, but my mixed emotions wouldn't let me leave like that. I needed Quamir to see the pain on my face, and then maybe he would understand what he was doing to me. I felt like I was in a trance, or better yet blazed; like everything was moving in slow motion, a euphoric high that made me feel like nothing was real. Nevertheless, I had to do this. I had to teach this chick a lesson about messing with my man or better yet, teach him a lesson about messing around on me.

Therefore, I pushed all rational thought out of my mind and let my heart and bruised emotions lead the way. I reached over Quamir's shoulder and yanked Shanice by the hair. All hell broke loose! I pounced on my prey like crazy, sending the entire porch into an uproar. I'm not sure how Quamir moved out of the way, but all I knew is that he was standing there watching as I dragged her down the stairs by her hair, causing parts of her weave to fly into the breeze.

"What I tell you about my man, trick!" I swung with all I had as I pulled her into the street. The flashing streetlamp that shone above us splashed like a spotlight into her frightened face.

"Toi!" Quamir screamed, running down the stairs, the soles of his Timberlands thumping against the wood. "Yo, chill."

Chill? To hell with chill—all chill could do for me at that moment was get its ass beat.

"What?" Tay said in killer mode. "I know you ain't tryna do nothin', Quamir!"

Quamir ignored her. Instead, he stood there watching with his left thumb tucked behind his belt buckle with a smirk on his face, all while I beat this girl down.

The girl threw a punch, but I ducked, came back up, and caught her in the chin.

"Shanice, Toi, I said chill," Quamir said with ease. I could tell he wanted to laugh because I could hear the sounds in his throat.

Although Shanice was trying to fight back, I was beatin' on her like crazy as Quamir stood there and watched as if this was his favorite pastime entertainment.

"Slap her!" Tay shouted. "Her face is clear again, Toi!"

"That's enough!" Seven yelled as she tried to pull me off of Shanice. Seeing that she wasn't successful, Quamir jumped in and lifted me up by my waist. Instantly, the fight ceased.

As Quamir put me down, he stood with his back to me as Shanice ran up and started pushing her chest against his. "Get out the way!"

My chest was heaving up and down. "Bring it!" I spat. "Bring . . . it!"

Tay shot me a high five, and wagged her tongue out like a salivating dog, "You . . . spank dat . . . ass!" she hunched her shoulders toward Shanice, who was still pushing against Quamir. "Booyah!"

"Yo," Quamir pushed Shanice back. "What I say?"

"Bring it! Please bring it!" I was screaming at the top of my lungs.

"Let me go, Quamir!" Shanice pushed against him and pointed at me. "I promise you, I'ma get you jumped, you ain't gon' never be able to walk these streets again! You really don't know who I am!"

"You ain't shit!" I yelled, "I just whooped yo' ass in front of your house and ain't nobody come out to help you? Girl, please."

"My mother ain't home, otherwise she'd would've shot yo' azz!"

I yawned, and tapped my lips, "What . . . eva!"

Shanice snorted, her weave hanging by a strand on her head. "You crazy bitch!" she struggled to reach for me, "I hate you! You know I'ma kill her, Quamir!"

"Chill," he said sternly.

"This yo' chick, Quamir?" I mushed him in the back of his head. "This your girl?"

"I'm his baby's mother, you stupid jump-off! He told you to step but you keep holding on!"

Did she just say baby mother? I looked at Tay for confirmation and her face went from confident and proud to surprised. Then I looked at Seven, who wore an "*I told you so*" face.

Whatever. How she gon' have a baby by him and I just had one? This chick lyin'. "He ain't never told me to step," I carried on. "You wish! And girl, you don't have no baby by him. Please!" *Of all things, I know Quamir wouldn't have no baby on me. We were a family; his other two baby mamas were crazy, I wasn't, which is why he told me I was the one.* I looked at Shanice, "Lose ya'self!"

"Oh, you ain't never told her about our son, Quamir?" Shanice said.

Son? I had the son.

"You ain't never told her to step, Quamir?" Shanice mushed Quamir in the face. "Oh, you her man?"

"What, you ain't know?" My words floated over his shoulder. "You better tell her somethin', Quamir."

"Quamir!" Shanice screamed.

"Quamir," I shouted. "Tell her, and tell her to stop lying on you!"

Quamir's head turned back and forth from me to Shanice over and over again. For a moment, he looked as if he were going crazy, but I didn't care. I desperately wanted him to validate what I was saying and straight out call this girl a liar.

"Quamir!" Shanice and I screamed simultaneously.

"Yo, for real," he snapped. "Both y'all gettin'

on my nerves! True story, I ain't rockin' wit' neither one of y'all like that."

For some reason, as if we were doing a dance,
we all stepped back. "What you say?" I think I
heard wrong.

"Oh, you ain't with me, Quamir?" Shanice spat.
"You been at my house every night this week and
we ain't together? You're the one who asked me
to have our baby so we would be a family—"

What she just say?

"And now," she continued on, "all of a sudden
you ain't with me?" She pushed him in his chest.
"Oh, we ain't together?"

He asked her what . . . ?

"Go 'head, Shanice." He pointed his finger in
her face.

My voice trembled as I said, "I can't believe
this!" I felt sooooo dumb. Here I was, battling with
a buncha lies, fighting for the sake of proving a
useless point.

"It's over, Quamir. This who you choosing?" I
pointed over his shoulder. "You can have that stank
ho! We through! You ain't nothin'; you don't take
care of your son no way. Mama's boy! Trying so
hard to be a playa but can't get outcha mama's
basement. Your whole existence is a joke. I don't
know whether to laugh in your face or spit in it."

I turned around to walk away, and Quamir
yanked me by my hair so hard that I was dizzy.
Seven and Tay immediately jumped between us. I
looked at the rage in Quamir's eyes and I knew he

wasn't playing. My heart thumped in my chest. "It's cool," I said to them as they stood in front of me.

"I been waitin' to kick yo' azz!" Tay said.

"Tay!" I snapped. "Chill. Y'all move and let me hear what he got to say." Before they could move on their own, Quamir pushed them to the side and stood in front of me.

"Who you talkin' to, Toi?" he said, sounding more like my father than my man.

I didn't answer.

"Don't you ever in your stupid life talk to me like that! You so stupid and dumb. This why don't nobody else want you! And no matter how I keep tryna stay with you, you keep actin' dumb! You need to get outta my business, retarded ho! You came around here actin' like a clown and all we gon' do is laugh at you."

"Don't be talking to her like that!" Seven screamed.

"You the stupid one!" Tay said.

"I know you ain't talkin' to me, you crazy ass, crack-head baby!" he spat with a sinister laugh.

"And what are you, Quamir?" Seven said. "At least Tay got an excuse."

Tay blinked her eyes. "Excuse me?"

"Ho, please," Quamir snorted. "I'm definitely not gon' argue with no virgin."

Feeling as if I was due to pass out at any minute, I fought with all I had to at least sound strong. "Boy, please. You been with this raggedy ho all week, and you talkin'!" The tears dancing in my throat stopped me mid-sentence. "This really yo' baby mama, Quamir?"

"Did I tell you I had another baby? Uh, answer me!"

Silence.

"Answer me!" he screamed.

"No!"

"Well then, why you assuming things?"

"What?" Shanice screamed, a flood of tears streaming down her face. "So what is you sayin'? That we don't have a son?" She punched him in his chest. "You sayin' he ain't yours?"

"Stupid tramp!" I tossed in the wind. "This broad really got a baby by you?" Suddenly, I felt like my son had been reduced to nothing. He wasn't the oldest, he wasn't the youngest, he wasn't even the one by the baby mama his daddy loved. He was just one of Quamir's kids. "You ain't nothing, Quamir! Matter of fact, it doesn't even matter what you do 'cause I'm out!"

"And I'm done with you, too." Shanice said. "I'm sick of you cheating on me!"

"Hos is always schemin'," Quamir said. "Man, please. Both y'all knew the deal and now you tryna act like you ain't know about the other? Now if you wanna stomp each other, then don't talk about it, be about it!" He stepped from in front of me. "What I care!"

Shanice started going off on Quamir, but I stood there. Stunned. Embarrassed. Wishing I could fly away and nobody would see me. Although he hadn't hit me, I felt like I'd been beaten. Why would he play me like this? What happened to him falling on his knees and telling this chick I was wifey?

I became anxious and didn't know what to do, where to turn, or how to act. I thought about crying but couldn't get any tears to come out. Then I thought about dying, but thinking of my son reminded me I had a reason to live. Then it hit me, I felt like nothing, as if all my wind had been sucked out and all that was left was a worthless shell.

"I'm leaving," Seven spat. "If you wanna stay here and take this crap, then do you, but me, I'm outta here!"

I stood there for a moment before walking backward to the car and getting in. I knew I looked crazy; I felt out of my mind. As the three of us got in the car and slammed the doors, I tried my best to believe what I was about to say. "I am so done with his ass!" I sniffed as tears covered my cheeks like glaze. "And I know he gon' come back beggin' me . . . like he always does. But I promise you, he gon' have to work real hard to get back with me. 'Cause I'm not beat for this no more!"

"You sound," Seven said, shaking her head as we drove off, "so damn dumb."

2

It was June and my room felt like a sweltering eighty degrees. My ceiling fan felt like it was doing nothing but making noise. Drops of sweat formed on my brow and my upper lip, and curled the edges of my flat ironed 'do.

I lay in the middle of my full-sized bed, my head underneath the pillow as the early morning sun rays covered my exhausted body. I had one arm swinging to the floor and the other thrown across my wide-awake, eight-month-old son, Noah, so he wouldn't fall out the bed.

Honestly, I just wanted a moment to cry. My life was a mess and all I kept thinking about was making things right with Quamir, even though I was the one who'd been mistreated.

Like, I knew he was dogging me. I wasn't blind;

I could see what he was doing to me. But so much of me felt like I was driven to stalk him, go through his things; listen to his voicemails, and anything else that continued to prove that he was no good.

"Easy-greasy," my sixty-year-old Cousin Shake yelled, scaring me out of my misery. He banged on my bedroom door, causing it to vibrate. "If you gon' slide down the pole with the hoochies at night, then you got to get up and catch the bus with the freaks in the mornin'."

I promise you I couldn't stand him. I wiped the tears from my eyes, marched over to the door and snatched it open.

"What, you wanna do somethin'?" He pushed up on me, then pretended to be holding himself back. "Don't hold me back. Please don't hold me back." I sucked my teeth. Every day he put on a show at my door. He skipped in place and the rainbow striped biking shorts he had on, with the loose jock (that he refused to let anyone explain to him went on the inside of his pants) bopped up and down along the middle of his thighs. And the four tires he had around his stomach all smacked each other like tuba beats, while his too-tight muscle shirt crept up his chest, scaring the hell outta me. Immediately, I started to scream and slammed the door in his face.

"Thought you ain't wanna do nothin'!" he said sounding as if he were trying to slither into my door crack. "Now get yo' azz up and get ready for work fo' I bust you upside the head." And just when I thought he was gone, he pounded on the door again.

"Yes!" I snapped.

"I cooked you some grits, they on the table."

"Thank you." I smiled. This was the only part I loved about his over-the-top ritual. "You love me, don't you, Cousin Shake?"

"You know I do. Now get dressed for work, fo' somebody gets hurt."

After I showered, I laid out my work uniform: a black hair net, white short sleeve shirt with IHOP stitched on the collar, a tight fitting black skirt, and a pair of throwback Pumas.

I walked into the kitchen with Noah, to prepare his bottles before I went to work.

"Hey Nana's man," my mother said as she took the baby from my hands and pointed to the clock. "Why are you still home? Haven't you gotten into enough trouble being late?"

I ignored that comment, especially since she worked her work schedule around mine, so that she could babysit (which was the only time I felt like she ever helped me out). I took a deep breath. "Good morning, ma."

Her eyes glanced at the clock. "It's close to being a good afternoon."

It was only ten o'clock in the morning. "I was up late last night." I tried to watch my tone.

"Of course you were. Crying over a no-good dog is hard work."

"Whatever," I mumbled.

"Yeah whatever, all I know is you better not come up in here without no job, because you chose to run the streets, and don't think that just because I don't see I don't hear."

Here we go . . .

"Alright Grier," Cousin Shake huffed his way into the kitchen. "I already done put it on her, she don't need no more."

To keep from snapping, I thought about humming, but since she was already wired and seemed to be looking for a reason to let me have it, I didn't hum.

"I know that's right," my mother said, shifting the baby from one hip to the other, "'bout time you learned to be quiet. I'll tell you this though. I'm tired of you and this Quamir nonsense. If you got to chase a man around in the street then—news flash, Toi—he doesn't want you."

That comment was a clear indication that my sister's been running her mouth . . . again.

"Oh," my mother continued on, "I spoke to my friend Phyllis, the caseworker at the welfare office, and she said they have a new program for teenage mothers in high school where they will pay for the daycare. I want you to go down there soon and apply."

"Okay ma." I just wanted to shut her up. "I will."

"I hope you didn't answer that quickly just to shut me up."

This was a no-win situation, so I simply said, "Bye," as I left out the room, heading for the bus stop.

3

I'd been working at IHOP part time, every day and every other weekend, for about six months.

As I pushed through the double glass doors the sweet aroma of pancakes and maple syrup floated through the air. The lobby was mad crowded and the floor was overflowing with customers. I was a few minutes late and my manager shot me the eye and pointed to his watch. I went in the back, placed my purse in my locker, and headed to my first table.

"Hey girl!" I waved at Tay, who was passing by me.

"Five o'clock, baby girl," she smiled, "five o'clock." Immediately, I looked to my right and there was a table full of cuties. "Either they college dudes or big ballers." She batted her eyes while waving hi to one of them. "I tried to take them off your hands and get them moved to my section, but you know Mr. Stick-Up-The-Ass," she pointed to our manager, "was all in my grill." She circled her hand in her face. "Needless to say, they all yours. Just save li'l Idris Elba, the one sitting in the corner, for me."

"Alright Tay." I turned toward the table and as soon as I made eye contact with the cutest one in the clan, I took a step and some kind of way I ended up splattered . . . all . . . over . . . the restaurant's floor.

"Help me." I heard a scratchy voice say from beneath me. "Please Jesus, save a pimp."

And when I looked down, I could've punched this dude in the face. It was Percy. Three and a half feet tall, Midget Mac, aka Percy Elwood Jenkins and two members of his too short crew: Cle'otis and Shim-daddy. And yes, Shim-daddy was his real name.

Be thankful that this crew wasn't in your 'hood, because I swear to you they were the world's best stalkers. Everywhere we went, they went. Following us, calling our names, tapping on our knees and begging us to please to go out with them. But Percy was the worst. And it wasn't because he was a dwarf either. Nobody paid any mind to that. It was because he was aggravating as hell, was always trying to get with somebody, and every time I looked at him, in the great words of Cousin Shake, he tore my eyes up.

He had a perm, Snoop Dogg curls in his hair, Lil Jon's glow in the dark grill (that spelled his name on the top row of his teeth), T-Pain's sweat socks to his knees, Andre 3000 plaid short-set, and Bishop Don Juan's rhinestone-studded-corduroy flip flops.

"Why is yo' li'l retarded ass," I said as Tay helped me up, "always in my way?"

"'Cause you want me in your way." Percy growled.

Instead of cussing him out, I crouched on my knees, squinted my nose, and barked like a German shepherd right in his face.

And in true Percy fashion, he passed out, spread out on the floor in front of all the customers like he was Jesus on the crucifix. I wanted to smack him. But instead I left him laying there.

"Psych homie. I was just playin'." He magically appeared before me. "But your breath was a little tart." He waved in front of his nose, "Don't worry, we can get you some Altoids and hook that up. Can't have you parading through the Little People's Convention and ya breath stink. People be like, 'there go Beyoncé, stank-ass breath and all.' "

God must be punishing me.

"My little brother," Tay rolled her eyes at Percy, "is the same size as you."

"Then ya mama need to bring him to see his daddy and stop playin'." He smiled and his mouth lit up. "Ask her what she waitin' on."

"Lil' Bootsy!" Percy's mother, who always seemed to appear out of nowhere, screamed. "Why are you always embarrassing me! Boy, get yo'self over here and sit down in this booster chair! And you better put this seat belt on. I swear I can't take you nowhere. You gon' mess around and I'ma have to bust you out. I see that comin'."

Me and Tay fell out laughing. "Ladies," my manager said in a warning tone, causing us to separate and service our customers. I walked over to the table of cuties.

"Welcome to IHOP. Would you like something to drink?"

"Nah," the king of cuties said. "Your number will do."

"973—" I said almost immediately without thinking. What the heck was I doing? Usually, I had more control then this. But damn, he was soooooo fine. And not that Chris Brown, pretty boy fine, but that rough rugged, 50 Cent fine, the kind of fine your mama doesn't want anywhere near your house, but you can't seem to do without. That kinda fine was right here in the flesh. He was like Juelz Santana . . . but finer. Six-two, tattoo on the side of his neck and a few sprinkled across his forearms, slanted eyes and thousands of spinning waves.

"What's good ma?" he asked. "You gon' finish hooking me up with the number or what?"

"Boy, please. I ain't thinking about you." I did all I could to suppress my blush. "You want something to drink or what?"

"Damn ma, you feeling me like that?"

"Yes—no . . . ." Why was I stuttering?

He stroked my hair away from my face and pushed it over my left shoulder, "You real pretty. You know that?"

I took a step back. This whole deal was a hot mess. I sucked my teeth. "Coke or Sprite?"

"Coke."

I wrote his order down and before I could get to his pot'nah, he said, "I'm Harlem. So what's your name?"

I ignored the question. "You wanna order your food now?"

He looked at my tag. "Toi. I like that."

"Me too."

One of the dudes sitting with him said, "Can I play with you?"

"Whatever." I blushed. "Are you ready to order or you still hooked on phonics?"

Harlem laughed, and oh what a cute laugh.

There were about three girls at the booth behind them who started snickering.

Harlem gave me a one-sided smile. "You wanna take this outside?"

"You threatening me?" I said jokingly.

"You want me to threaten you?"

"I do. You can threaten me."

Tay, who was standing behind me, turned away from her customer and said, "And you can threaten me." She started pointing around the table, "and you, and you, oh, and definitely *you*. You can threaten me any way you want."

"Tay," I said, tight-lipped. "Stop it."

"Oh." She smiled and turned back toward her customer. "Hollah."

"Ai'ight, ma," Harlem said. "Ask my boy what he orderin'. I ain't sure yet."

I looked at him out the corner of my eye. "Whatever." Was I still blushing? I looked at the dude sitting next to him. "What you orderin'?"

He pointed to Harlem, "The same thing he is, but if I can't get that, I'll take one of your friends on the side."

"Somebody call me?" Tay practically tripped over to the table. "I mean," she said, straightening her apron out, "I'm here . . . " She stared at one of Harlem's friends. "Dang boy, is Idris Elba yo' daddy? 'Cause you fine as hell."

"Thank you." The guy blushed. "But my name is Ibn."

"Heyyyy," Tay said with a twang. "You like the moon—the stars—and all that shit put together. You so fine, I know yo' daddy pretty."

"Tay," I said again, still tight-lipped.

"I'm just sayin'." She smiled. "Just keepin' it real—hollah!"

"Why don't you keep this real?" Sounded over my shoulders. Instantly, my heart started thundering in my chest. I turned around and Quamir was standing there. Immediately, I took a step back.

Quamir looked Harlem dead in the face. "Listen, li'l dude. Unless you looking to get hurt, you'll back away from my girl. 'Cause trust and believe, you don't want none of me."

Harlem laughed as he looked at Quamir. "Is this the part where you want me to be scared or what?"

"What you say, pot'nah?" Quamir snapped, obviously caught off-guard. "'Cause I will put a cap right in your ass. Try me. I ain't nothin' to play with."

Harlem looked at Quamir like he was stupid. "Whatever, man."

"I got your whatever, man. You better relax and step away from my girl."

Harlem frowned. "'Let me kick this to you real quick. Unless you gon' take her out of here now and have her follow you around, telling me you're her man doesn't mean shit to me, 'cause everywhere and every time I see her I'ma kick it to her and that very day she's missing and you're wondering where she is," Harlem slipped the pen out my hand and wrote a phone number down on a napkin, "call me and I'll be sure to let you hollah at her for a minute."

"Oh damn," Tay said. "What's really good?"

"Shut up." I looked at her.

"You talkin' all that," Quamir spat, "but I betchu he won't take it outside."

"Not right now," Harlem said, "'cause I'm 'bout to order my food. But when I step out that door and you bring it outside, then it's whatever." He looked at me. "Now, can I place my order?"

"Yes," I looked down at my order pad, hoping Quamir would get the hint to leave. "What would you like?"

"Oh, you just gon' take his order right in front of me?"

I'm a waitress. What does he expect me to do? Usually I would've taken this on, but this time I ignored him. I couldn't lose my job because I had to take care of my son. It was a rare occasion that anybody besides my mother helped me do that.

"Oh ai'ight, Toi. This how we rollin'?" Quamir asked in disbelief.

I turned to him. "Baby," I said as soft as I could, "please let me work. Give me five minutes and I'll meet you outside."

"Five minutes? Oh, I ain't good enough for right now? I got to wait five minutes to be somethin' around here?"

He was embarrassing the heck outta me. "Sweetie, please," I said as nice as I could, doing everything in my power not to cause a scene.

"That's all you gettin' too is five minutes." And he stormed out.

I didn't even turn to look at him. I guess he expected me to drop everything and run behind him. Well, how was I gon' do that when I needed my job? I mean, yeah I loved him, and yeah I'll go hard for him, but I need my money—especially since he stopped giving me any a long time ago. Besides, why was he at my job anyway? Last I checked, he was playing me to the left in the middle of Rector Street.

Once I served Harlem and his friends their orders, I asked my manager if I could get a break and he said no, I had to wait for my scheduled time, which was forty-five minutes later.

Between serving my customers and looking outside, I could see Quamir watching me from the parking lot. I glanced at the clock and my break was coming up soon. I picked up a few tips from the empty tables and checked on several of my customers before I was finally able to step outside.

I took a deep breath as I headed over to Quamir's truck.

"You a comedian now, huh?" he said, sounding ridiculous. "Don't you ever have me waitin' like this again!" He grabbed me by my collar.

I slapped his hand. "Get offa me! I couldn't go on break."

"You couldn't go on break," he said as his hand fell, "but you could find time to talk to playboy. You must think I'm stupid. You couldn't give me five minutes but ole boy can get your whole lifetime."

"What are you talking about? I was doing my job!" My throat started to swell with tears. "Did you really have a baby on me?"

"Don't try and change the subject. Who was that dude? I told you I ain't like that dude and you still hanging around him."

"He's a customer. I can't tell him to stop coming here."

"Oh, now you got new customers?"

"What?"

"I thought I was your number one customer?"

"And I thought you were my boyfriend!"

"So you admit you're cheating on me?"

"What?" I was confused.

"So you don't have nothing going on with this dude? Never? Ever?"

"No."

"Now you lyin'—you told me y'all went together in the third grade."

"I never said that! I said I went with a dude named June in third grade."

"Well damn, how many cats you kicking it with? You just a ho, huh?"

"I'm not a ho. Your mama's a ho. She's the one who gave birth to a pimp."

Quamir mushed me on the side of my head. "What you say? That's exactly why we ain't back together, 'cause Shanice is more of a woman than you'll ever be." He palmed my face and knocked me to the ground. "Stupid ass!"

He hopped in his truck and sped off, the screeching tires leaving smoke behind.

I did all I could not to cry. I cleared my throat and tried to smooth out the wrinkles in my uniform. I sniffed, and as I turned to go inside, Harlem was standing there. "You know you don't deserve to be treated like that."

"It's not what you think."

"I know Toi." He sighed. "It never is."

"You don't understand. He's going through something."

"Whatever you say ma." He fixed my collar. "I left my number on the table. Hollah at me when you get it together."

4

—

I'd called Quamir a million times this morning and he hadn't answered not even once. Every time I heard his voicemail, I got sick to my stomach. I kept wondering what he's doing, who's he's with, and why he's treating me like this. And then I'd get pissed that no matter how hard I tried, I couldn't seem to let this relationship go. It was sooooo obvious that this was a dead end street, yet I kept going around and around, ignoring all the signs that told me I needed to break out.

And it's not like I loved Quamir the same way I did when things were good. He was perfect then. He gave me money and bought me clothes—and not no regular department store shit, either. Classy shit, shit that chicks around here couldn't even pronounce, let alone afford. I was that girl every ho wanted to be and now look at me. My all-starhood-hustlin' boyfriend had turned into a no-good baby daddy; I was on welfare; and my mother was on my back about everything. If it wasn't for Tay, I'd be catching the bus everywhere, and yeah, I'm still cute—don't get it twisted—but I couldn't afford a thing that Qua used to buy me, so I'm limited to places like The Gap.

"Toi," my mother knocked on my bedroom door and opened it at the same time. "Why haven't you gone and applied for that childcare program like I told you?"

I rolled my eyes to the ceiling. "I forgot."

"I swear." She shook her head. "Well, you need to get up and go down to the welfare office right now. Today is the last day."

I sucked my teeth. Can someone please tell her that I hate the word welfare? "But I have to go to work."

"Oh, you're going." She placed her hand on her hip. "But you're going to the welfare office to apply for this child care program first. Like I told you to last week. This way Noah can be in daycare in September and you don't have to worry about a babysitter."

"Alright ma, I get the point."

"I hope so. Now, I'll take him with me this morning. I'm going to visit your Aunt Gerri."

"You're off today?"

"Yes I am." She took the baby out of his crib and walked out of my room.

I swear I'd hit rock bottom. This whole deal

was something I'd never imagined. I always thought you had to be poor, down and out with little to nothing, or just plain lazy to get welfare benefits.

I shook my head. I couldn't get sad about this shit. I had to choke it up. Quamir had caused me to be sad enough and I didn't need to bring anything more on myself.

I got out of my bed, showered, and threw on a pink BeBe sweat suit, matching kicks, pulled my hair in a single ponytail, slid on my D&G round-eyed shades and went on my way.

When I entered the welfare office, I was pissed at all the people waiting in line. I knew my manager was gon' flip; there was no way I would be on time today.

I signed my name underneath the fifty million other people waiting to see a caseworker and I sat down. There were crying children and complaining adults everywhere. For a moment I felt like I was going crazy. People were being paged over and over again on the loudspeaker and the security guard was arguing with a new client every five minutes. There were a thousand different safe sex posters, AIDS, suicide, depression hotline numbers, and information about welfare fraud.

And if that wasn't enough, there were about a zillion different songs floating through the air from the radio on the security guard's desk, to the elevator music in the lobby, to the clients' mundane songs: *I can't believe they cut my benefits . . . I wish these people would come on. They tryna say my kids don't even live with me. I need my money. Where my food stamps? I lost my card. I found my card. I ain't goin' to no damn Work-First program . . ."* And on and on it went until I felt like my head was spinning.

I got up and walked from one end of the lobby to the next. By the time I came back, someone had taken my seat. I decided it wasn't worth the drama of asking this person to move, so I just leaned against the wall until my name was called.

"Ms. McKnight." A caseworker I'd never seen before called my name. She held the door open for me to come in and introduced herself. "I'm Mrs. Smith and I've just been assigned your case."

"Oh, what happened to Ms. Roberts?"

"She quit."

"Oh, well I was coming to apply for the new daycare program for teenage mothers."

"You have to be in school."

"I am."

She looked at me funny. "I don't mean a G.E.D. program."

"Excuse me? Did I say I was in a G.E.D. program?"

"I'm just letting you know." She opened my folder. "Are you aware that you have to update your benefits?"

"Why?"

"All your information is not completed and if you don't complete it then we will cut off your Medicaid and the money you get every month."

I looked at her like she was crazy. "I don't get money every month."

She looked surprised. "You have a job?"

"Yes." I snapped.

"Through the Work First program?"

"No."

"Oh . . . Well, if you make more than three hundred dollars a month, then we'll be cutting your food stamps."

"I didn't apply for food stamps." She was pissing me off.

"So what do you need? Housing? The only place we can offer you is the homeless hotel. Otherwise, I don't know what to tell you."

"Are you listening to me?" I snapped. "I said the new childcare program."

"Fine, then I need some updated information on your child's father because we don't have any. Do you know his name?"

"What?"

"His real name, not Pooky, Saboo, Supreme, Dream, or whatever else they are calling themselves these days. I mean his birth name or government name as you all call it."

I wanted to slap her. "It's Quamir Lewis."

"His mother's name?"

"Huh?"

"Your child's grandmother's name."

I sat there for a moment. "I don't know."

"Okay," the worker said as if this was beyond familiar. "Mr. Lewis's date of birth."

"June 1, 19 . . . 85 . . ." I said, more like a question than a statement. "I mean, 86."

"His social security number?"

"I don't know that." I felt like a complete fool. "Listen, why do you need all of this just to apply for childcare? I gave all of this information before."

"Perhaps, but the information here is not complete."

I promise you I wanted to punch her in the face. "That's all I know."

"Do you have a current address and his job information?"

"No."

"Well, Ms. McKnight, we need his information because he has to pay child support."

"I don't have it."

"We need your cooperation."

"I understand. When I find out something, I will let you know."

"Thank you," she shuffled the papers. "I appreciate that. Oh," she handed me a stack of paperwork, "you need to fill these out for the childcare program. And we need copies of two paycheck stubs."

"Uhm hmm," I said. "Sure."

She nodded her head and I got up and left. For some reason I felt like only an hour or so had gone by, but when I looked at the clock, I realized three hours had passed. I walked to the bus stop and leaned against the rail. I had to get out of this existence. Things had to change; somehow, some way, I needed my life to be different. I didn't have a boyfriend, I didn't have a life. I had nothing but menial work hours and embarrassing welfare benefits.

I caught the bus home, changed into my uniform and headed to work. As I stepped into IHOP, my cell phone rang. It was Quamir. "Hello?" I said, not knowing what to expect.

"Wassup?" he said as if nothing had ever happened between us, a sure sign that he wanted to work things out.

"Nothing, working," I said, standing in the lobby before going into the back and checking on my station.

"Oh, ai'ight. Well, when you get off, come through."

I blushed. "Why?"

"'Cause I wanna see you."

"Sure?"

"I'm more than sure."

That made my day and I knew my work hours would fly by. I made up my mind that this time I was going to get things right. Sure, Quamir had cheated and what he did wasn't easy to accept, but I'd played my part in pushing him out there. I nagged too often, expected too much, and was always complaining about things. So this time, none of that would be going on. If I wanted peace and a relationship with my son's father, then I had to be on my best behavior.

After completing my shift, I caught the bus to Quamir's house. As the back doors of the bus opened, revealing Quamir's stoop, I saw his ex-girlfriend, Desha, sitting there. Immediately, we locked eyes and she gave me a look that said we were thinking the same thing, *What is she doing here?*

Before I could collect my thoughts, Quamir walked so swiftly toward me that I practically fell backwards. "Yo', wassup?" he said.

"What is she doing here?" I pointed behind him.

"You know how chicks is, always tryna come through without calling."

I knew he was lying. I could just tell. "So tell her to go home."

"Nah, I don't wanna be rude. Her father just died."

"And what does that have to do with you?"

"Look," he said, flicking his nose, "let me hollah at you later. I'll call you when she leaves and then you can come back through."

I stood there for a moment. "Excuse me? You invited me here and now you want me to leave because she's here . . . unexpectedly?"

"See, you don't listen," he snapped.

"What?"

"Just go home."

"I can't keep going through this! First Shanice and now this chick. How many others is it?"

"Yo'," he smirked, "you can either play your position or change your position. I already told you she came by for a minute and I'll hit you up when she's gone. Ai'ight?"

Tears welled in my eyes but I couldn't cry. At that moment I realized nothing was going to change. Nothing. And no matter what I did, Quamir would always be the same. "You know what, maybe you're right," I said.

"Finally, she gets it," he said, sarcastically.

"Yeah, and maybe I need to fall back, fall all the way back."

He rolled his eyes to the sky. "Here we go again."

"Here we go again?" I said in disbelief. "I am so serious. We are really over."

He yawned and stretched his arms. "Alright, Toi. Whatever you say."

I was in complete awe. "Quamir . . . you really don't care?"

"Look, what you want from me, a trophy, a ride or die prize or something? Every time I turn around, you always leaving, you always doing this, that and the third. And you ain't gon' do nothin' but call me on the phone cryin'. Man, whatever. Like I told you when you were fighting Shanice, you not my girl, so if you wanna bounce, then do you. But don't try and stunt and play me 'cause I got company. Yeah, I called you over here and now I'm telling you to go home. Dig? Now be out."

And he left me standing there. I looked at his porch and Desha pleasantly watched the whole thing. I could tell she got the biggest kick out of him playing me. I wondered for a moment if I'd died and gone to hell. But then I realized that this was my life and that I couldn't and wouldn't do this anymore. A part of me wanted to run up on Quamir and beat him down or ask him why. Why was he doing this? But how many times was I going to ask the same thing? It was official. I was tired of the drama, at least this type of drama. I had to get out, I needed to get away, otherwise loving this dude was clearly going to make me crazy. There was a bus coming up the street, it wasn't even the right bus that would take me home, but I didn't care. I just had to get away from here. I stepped on the bus and figured I would go for a ride and when I decided to find my way home, I would.

Drama Part II

Fly Like Me . . .

5

It was July 4th weekend, the block association was giving a slammin' outdoor pool party, and cuties were everywhere. Chingy's "Fly Like Me" was bumpin' and me and my girls were funky, fresh, and fly to death. Needless to say, it was now ... (drum roll please) ... officially on.

As we strolled along the crowded pool side with water splashing at our feet, me, Seven, and Tay gleamed like America's next top model.

And yeah, Seven and Tay looked cute but my gear was puttin' all the hoochies to sleep: Hot pink bikini halter, hip hugging Daisy Dukes (with the snap and zipper open, showing the top portion of my bikini bottom), BeBe kitten heel thongs, Aviator shades, pink bangles clapping down my right arm and a cherry Blow Pop in my mouth.

"So what's the game plan?" said Tay, who popped

her lips every time she spoke, as we eyed the assortment of tenders. "'Cause I need my hair and nails done."

"I was thinking the same thing." Seven laughed while twirling one of Tay's deflated curls.

"Don't hate, Seven," Tay rolled her eyes. "It is so unattractive . . . But for real though, who we checkin' for?" She pointed to the cats with Tims, jeans and R.I.P. spray painted on their white tees. "Ballers?"

"Girl, please." I blinked my eyes a series of times. "Ain't nobody messin' with those ghetto birds."

"Fa' sho'." Seven jerked her neck, blew a pink bubble and popped it. "I already have a boo, but if I didn't, I wouldn't wanna date nobody with a homie dying every week."

"True," Tay agreed, "'cause last year I was meeting all my new boos at funerals." Her eyes started a new scan. "Okay, how about shot callers?" she pointed to the dudes with the too-tight swimming trunks and their bare feet slapping against the concrete.

"Can you say bootie chokers and athlete's feet?" I snapped in disbelief that Tay even suggested that.

She sucked her teeth. "Let's see," she pointed again. "Brawlers?"

"Repeat after me," Seven spoke slowly, "Juvenile . . . Detention . . . Center . . . Parolees."

"Puleeze, puleeze. . .ah puleeze . . ."

"Y'all standards too high," Tay said, aggravated.

"And that's exactly why you need to look down here," growled up from my knees. I should've known that it was too good to be true: I was in the hood and hadn't seen a roach all day. Psyched my mind, because here was the roach that never died: Percy Elwood Jenkins and his crew, Cle'otis and Shim-daddy.

"I don't have time for this." Tay sucked her teeth.

"Me either," Seven said as her attention was distracted by her boyfriend, Josiah, who'd just walked in. "There go my boo."

"And he got friends with him," Tay raced behind Seven as I continued to try and get away.

"But Toi—" Percy ran in front of me.

"Nope." I wiggled my neck and tried again to walk away, again.

"Nope? You didn't let me finish. I was sayin'—"

"Not gon' happen." And once again I tried to escape, but my legs were surrounded.

"What's not gon' happen—"

"Me and you, that's what!"

"Girl, you know you want me!" Percy screamed and don't you know this fool had the nerve to have an attitude? "I don't even know why you fightin' it," he carried on, "you know I'm hot," he pounded his chest, "delicious and nutritious, er'-body want a taste of this tender crisp."

"Lil' Bootsy!" Ms. Minnie, Percy's mother, lifted up the living room window and screamed his nickname. They lived next door to the community pool. As a matter of fact, they lived so close that you could be in their house and have your feet in the pool at the same time. She slapped the palm of her hand with a rubber slipper. "Lil' Bootsy, get yo' fake ass playboy behind in this house and wash these dishes! Left my dern kitchen a mess!"

"Mama, why you got to act like that?" He looked around, and if I ain't know any better, I would think this fool was embarrassed. "And stop calling me Lil' Bootsy!"

"Percy Elwood Jenkins," Ms. Minnie snapped, "who in the bubble gum ass you talkin' to? You better break yo'self fool, and recognize!"

"I guess I can leave now, Lil' Bootsy." I rolled my eyes and the next thing I knew, Percy had tripped me and I was headed for the pool face first . . . oh . . . my . . . God!

"Whooaa ma!"

Someone's large masculine arm wrapped around my waist, attempting to save me from the water, only for him to fall in right behind me. So much for Brick City having a superman. You know I was pissed, right? "The least you could've done," I said as I wiped the water from my eyes and blocked out the shock, surprise, and laughter of the people around me, "was not fall in behind me. You just made it worse. At least I could've played it off by myself."

"Excuse you? Was that a thank you? 'Cause technically I ain't have to do nothin' for you. Last I checked, you weren't my girl."

Immediately, I looked up. I'd know that voice anywhere. Harlem. I swear I was melting in his arms. But wait . . . hold it . . . didn't he just read me? Yeah, I believe he did. "Excuse you, Uptown, but you can calm down." Don't ask me how, but some kind of way my arms slid around his thick neck and my fingers locked. "'Cause last I checked, I didn't ask to be your girl."

"You should've called." He gave a me a sexy look, his eyes meeting mine half staff while he looked down at me. "Maybe you would be my girl by now."

"Yeah, right."

"So, you still wit' ole boy?"

"Psst, please. That boy was hella crazy."

"Is that a no?"

"Of course it's a no."

"Ai'ight." He smiled, "so why didn't you call me?"

"Because—"

"Because what?"

"I don't know." What the hell was I talking about? I knew good and well if this dude asked me to marry him, I was gon' do it. "Look . . . maybe . . . I should go. Thank you for trying to help me."

"Where are you going?" he pulled me back to him.

I stared at him, trying to figure out why I was trippin' over him so hard.

"What you thinking about?" He stroked my cheek. "A minute ago, you were Miss Fresh and Fly and now you melting in my arms."

Heck, I've been melting in your arms. "Nothing." I shook my head, my wet hair splashing against my shoulders. "I wasn't thinking about anything."

He laughed, "Still at IHOP, right?"

"Yeah."

"I'ma come through tomorrow."

"Alright." I went to pull away again and he pulled me back.

"What?" He placed my arms back around his neck. "You got something against chilling right now?"

I wondered if this was too good to be real. "Nah, nothing's wrong with us . . . chilling right now."

"Straight." He kissed me on my forehead and I almost passed out amidst my kitten heels, shades, and Blow Pop floating in the water. He rubbed the sides of my hair to the back and we started kicking it. Just like that. In the middle of the pool, as if we were always supposed to be here, with my hair slicked down like silk, my Daisy Dukes soaking wet, and the DJ playing Teedra Moses' "Be Your Girl," the very song that I just realized was spilling all of my secrets.

6

"Okay," Tay said as she drove us to work. "How big, how long, and don't spare any details."

"What," I paused and looked at her, "are you talking about?"

"You know—Harlem's Tarzan, his Johnson, the pipe!"

"You are soooo nasty." I laughed. "I don't believe you. I know you don't think he was getting more than a free feel in the pool? I am not a ho."

"And you ain't a virgin either, so spill it."

"It was nothing. We just kicked it."

"So you feelin' him?"

I blushed. "Yeah, he's cute."

"It's obvious that he's cute. I said, are you feelin' him?"

"I don't know him."

"Okay," she turned the corner, "let me say it like this. Are you over Quamir?"

"Girl, please. Ain't nobody thinking about Quamir," I lied Although each day I thought about him less and less, I still thought about him. "Life goes on without Quamir."

"Does he call about the baby?"

"No."

"Typical."

"Exactly."

"Oh," she said a little too excited as we pulled into the IHOP parking lot. "I knew I had something to tell you."

"What?"

"Remember Ronnique from my home room last year?"

"There were two Ronniques. Which one?" My silver bangles jingled down my right arm as I opened the door and got out.

"I *said* my homeroom," she stressed as we walked toward the building and walked in.

"Oh, yeah. I remember."

"Okay, well Quiera, who lives in my building, told me that Ronnique is best friends with Deeyah."

"So," I sucked my teeth long and hard, sounding just like my West Indian grandmother. "And?"

"You'll never guess who Deeyah's god-sister is."

"Who?"

"Shanice."

"Who?"

"The broad you beat up, the one Quamir was messing with."

"For real?"

"Fa sho', and guess what else?" She popped her eyes wide.

"What?"

"She a ho."

The biggest smile in the world ran across my face. Finally, Tay had good news. "How you know?"

"'Cause Ronnique told me. Apparently, Shanice was asking Deeyah did she know you and it went from there. You know how chicks talk. Anywho, according to their li'l crew, Shanice doesn't know whose baby that really is and she just put him on Quamir because she thought he was some stand-up cat or something like that. But *booyah*, she found out he wasn't crap just like them other tricks."

"Excuse you?"

"You know what I mean." She winked her eye. "So maybe that ain't Quamir's seed after all."

We looked at the restaurant's employee board and made mental notes of our stations.

"It doesn't even matter," I grabbed a pen and order pad. "Quamir can roll over and die for all I care. We are through."

Tay rolled her eyes toward the ceiling, "Toi, it's me. Tay. You don't have to lie to me."

"I'm serious."

Tay shook her head. "I just can't believe you haven't heard from him."

"I've given up. I don't even care anymore."

"Why?" Tay teased. "'Cause you sweatin' Harlem?"

"You are such a hater." I laughed.

"I don't hate… I state—"

"Anyway," I cut her off. "You know I got the dances from Beyoncé's "Get Me Bodied," down pat. I puts 'em all to sleep."

"Yeah, right." Tay snickered. "You should've seen me, Seven, and Shae the other night at The Arena. It was teen night and we were off the hook!"

"The Arena?" I was taken aback. "Y'all went to The Arena and didn't invite me?"

"Every time we ask, you can never go."

I had an attitude. "I don't believe this."

"Don't be mad. We didn't want you to feel bad, so we didn't say anything. Don't be mad."

I fostered a smile and did my best to push my hurt feelings to the side. "I'm good. For real, it's cool."

"So, can you show me the dance? I been trying to learn it forever."

"We need to get to the floor. You know the manager gon' bug in a minute."

"No, he's not." Tay insisted. "We have a few minutes."

"Okay, you show me first what you were doing the other night. And if we have time, I'll show you what I can do."

"Bet." She started breaking it down and as I watched her, I wondered if I could ever recapture the way she must feel: carefree, not bogged down with adult responsibilities, able to do what she wanted with her money and not have to worry about milk and Pampers. I wanted to feel like that again. Like a regular teenager on top of the world, like nothing else mattered but what I wanted to do. And just as I was beginning to feel like I was almost there and could touch it, our manager walked in the back and yelled, "Ladies, you have customers waiting!" and I was forced to come back to reality.

7

"**A**aaaaaaaaahhhhhh!" My brother screamed at the top of his lungs. "What the hell is this?"

My mother stormed down the hall. "I know this boy ain't cussin' in my house!"

Welcome to Sunday morning at the McKnights' crib. This was our before-church ritual; my mother would pick out my brother's clothes and he would lose his mind because he hated them every time. Thank God I had to work—well, actually I didn't have to work. I just lied so that I didn't have to go to church and I could have peace of mind, go back to sleep, and then maybe go to the mall or something.

As I packed Noah's bag for him to go with my mother, I heard her yell, "Man-Man, you cussin' up in here?"

"Damn shame," Cousin Shake said. "Not even

on a Sunday morning can these skeezoids give their nasty-ass mouths a rest!"

"I don't care what you say," Man-Man insisted. "I ain't wearing this!"

"I tell you what," my mother spat, "if you don't wear that suit, then you will not be having a Kool-Aid stand."

"Ma," he held his arms out, and the cuffs of his sleeves raised half way up his arms. "Look at me . . . look . . . at . . . me. You know this is too small and why, why do I have to keep wearing fire trucks, dogs, and cop cars on my clothes? I'm ten years old ma. All the kids gon' tease me if the cuff of my sleeve slapping me in the head!"

"You look adorable."

"I look stupid!"

"It's worse than that," I added, walking into the kitchen with Noah on my hip.

My mother shot me the evil eye. "You look like a respectable young man."

"Kids don't know good clothes when they see 'em!" Cousin Shake yelled. "In my day, we made clothes out of leaves."

"And you still wearin' 'em, too!" Man-Man yelled at Cousin Shake.

Cousin Shake blinked in disbelief, then looked around and started skipping in place. "Don't hold me back. Please don't hold me back!"

"I'm not wearing this!" Man-Man started undressing and in an instant he stood there showing off his fake tattoo of blond chest hairs and his

57

royal blue Superman underwear. "I'm tired of reppin' for 5-0. You like it so much, you wear it! But since you insist that I gotta go to church and you won't let me change my clothes, then this is how I'm going." He poked out his chest. "I'm wearing exactly what I got on."

I just shook my head because I knew what was next. WHAP!!!BAM!!!BOOM!!! And like magic Man-Man was dressed. My mother grabbed the baby and they headed out the door. "Play with me if you want some, too!" my mother said, closing the front door behind her.

I ran into my room and watched them pull off down the street. Then I walked over to my bed and fell backwards on to it. Ahhhh, I couldn't believe this. This was magical. I could go back to sleep, and when I woke up, sneak to the mall. Now, this was what I call Sunday morning worship. I picked up the remote to my AC, snuggled under the covers, and let my head melt into the pillow.

"I think Josiah is cheating on me!" made me jump out of my sleep. My heart felt like it was racing as Seven, Tay, and Seven's best friend Shae swung my door open and stood at the foot of my bed. "Wake up!" Seven screamed. "Did you hear what I said?"

They had to be crazy, they had to be. I didn't even respond. Instead, I took my pillow, covered my face and let out a muffled scream. All I wanted was some sleep and here . . . she reintroduced me to misery.

Tay snatched the pillow off my face. "Your sister has an emergency!"

"Jesus!" I said as if I had a seventy-year-old body that ached. "Jesus!"

"You're so selfish!" Shae snapped. "Always have been."

I sighed with my eyes still closed. "Y'all better stop playing with me."

"We're not," Seven sucked a glob of snot back into the bridge of her nose and plopped down on the edge of my bed.

I opened my eyes and shook my head.

"I really think Josiah is cheating on me," she said.

"Sounds that way to me," Tay insisted.

I sighed. "And why is that?" Apparently this was the part where I was supposed to be patient and forget about my own problems or something like that. "What's been going on?"

"You know I'm still a virgin."

"The whole world knows that, Seven," Tay said. "Tell her something new."

"Taylor," I said, tight-lipped, calling Tay by her whole name. "Be quiet."

"I'm just saying."

"Hush," Shae said. "Let her talk." She rubbed Seven's back. "Go 'head, Seven."

"Well, for the last month he hasn't asked for any booty."

I wanted to scream, 'cause *he got tired of you saying no!* But instead I said, "So?"

"So?" They all said simultaneously.

"So?" I said for confirmation. "And?"

"You're her twin," Shae said, "you're supposed to feel her pain."

"And all you have to say is *so?*" Tay scrunched her top lip.

I promise you I just wanna take the back of my hand and slap these broads. "What . . ." I spoke slowly, "happened?"

Seven wiped her eyes. "I went up to his school and his bags were packed."

"Typical niggah," Tay snapped, "tryna sneak out on a bitch."

"Was all that called for?" I looked at her. "You need to stop getting people all hyped up." I turned my attention back to Seven. "So what if his bags were packed. It's the summer time."

"But he's in the basketball program—they stay until the end of July."

"Did you ask him where he was going?"

"No, I just saw some chick staring at me like I was crazy. And then there were these dudes and the next thing I know Josiah was gone and he didn't even say goodbye. No kiss, no whisper about when I was going to give him some. Nothing. And then he calls and suddenly gives me a new address saying he moved off campus."

Now this caught my attention.

"He's living with some slut," Tay said. "I betchu."

"Then why would he give her the address?" Shae asked.

"I don't know." Tay hunched her shoulders. "I don't have all the answers."

I sat straight up. "You said it was a chick?"

"And dudes." Seven cried.

"Forget about the dudes, unless you think . . . we're dealing with some down low freaky-deaky stuff."

"I ain't even think of that, Toi," Tay said. "That is true."

"Heck no, my boo ain't on the low-low!" Seven yelled.

"That's what they all say," Tay insisted. "But for real for real, it's a whole lotta dudes walking around with hydraulics in their pants. One minute they're up and without warning," she dropped to the floor in a Beyoncé bounce, "they done dropped down."

"Get up." I looked at Tay like she was crazy.

"Not Josiah." Seven sniffed.

"Okay, so back to the chick," I said. "She was looking at you crazy?"

"Yeah," she answered.

"And this is the first time Josiah hasn't asked for any booty?"

"It's been going on for a month."

"A whole . . . entire month?" Tay snapped. "My Gawd, break that down for me now, you said one month?"

"Thirty days," Seven said. "Seven hundred and twenty hours, forty-three thousand, two hundred minutes—"

"And a whole lotta seconds—" Tay added.

"That he ain't asked her for no booty," Shae interjected. "We got a problem."

"Oh . . . my . . . God . . ." I stood up.

"You see my point?" Seven cried.

"Hell yeah," Tay's eyes popped out. "He playin' the hell outta you!"

"I don't believe Josiah." Shae shook her head.

"Why didn't you tell me this earlier?" I asked her.

"I don't know."

"Well," Tay sucked her teeth, "we gon' have to roll up on him and bust him out."

Immediately, Seven broke down. "I knew it."

"Shut up cryin' now." Tay started pacing. "If you roll up on Josiah cryin', he gon' think you a weak punk."

"I'm not no punk." She wiggled her neck.

"I know you ain't 'cause you my girl!" Shae encouraged Seven. "Hmph, the Hottie Posse. We steal, we don't get stole on."

Tay threw a punch into the air. "That's right."

"Shoot, they don't know about me," Seven snapped.

"I know they don't." I said—I was getting hyped up, too.

"I betchu . . . I betchu . . . if I open my wallet my ID gon' say bad mamma-jamma."

"There it is." We all exchanged high-fives. "So get dressed," they looked at me, "and you know, Shae," Tay said, "since Melvin and Josiah are friends, then Melvin and his country behind just might be on the creep-creep too."

"You think so?" Shae said, getting upset.

"Hmph, you never know."

It was official—we had to wreck shop. But don't get it twisted, although we were pissed, not being cute was not an option. So we all worked cargo capris. Tay had on denim, I had on khaki, Seven had on blue, and Shae wore red. And we all wore fitted wife-beaters with leopard push-up bras underneath, showing just a little of the cup. We also wore stilettos but don't sleep, sneakers were in our bags, along with some Vaseline, and a place to slide our earrings, if need be.

Afterwards, we headed out the door and piled into Tay's hatchback Civic. And in true Tay fashion, she had DMX's "Where My Dogs At" on repeat. This, of course, hyped us up even more. Once we arrived at Josiah's new address, Tay parked the car and said, "Now don't get in there acting stupid," she instructed Seven and everybody agreed. "Our mission is to go in there, break this fool and let him know you ain't the one. We already know you the world's oldest virgin, but that don't give him the right to cheat on you."

"I'm not the world's oldest virgin!" Seven snapped.

"Ain't nothin' wrong with that. Maybe you can be a nun or something," Tay said.

"I'm not trying to be no nun!" Seven screamed.

"And what's wrong with being a nun?" I snapped.

"At least you don't have to go to college for that. It'll get mommy off your back. You know she ain't gon' play with God."

"Be quiet," Shae said. "Her being stingy with the booty is not the problem, 'cause it didn't stop Quamir from dogging you!"

"You snapping on me?"

"No," was her attempt to clean it up. "I was just making a point."

"Well don't make it over here."

"Stop it!" Seven screamed, causing all of us to jump and look at her like she was crazy. "My life is coming to an end and you all are arguing!"

"You ain't gon' be yelling at me!" Tay rolled her neck. "Shoulda just gave him some and you wouldn't be in this mess."

We fixed our clothes as we headed up the steps. The bass in the music coming from inside the house was so loud that the hip-hop song they were playing was unrecognizable. There were Greek letters on the front of the building that actually looked to be an old brownstone painted yellow and gold. There was also a bulldog on the front door. "Look, Seven," Tay said, "he just rubbin' it all in your face."

I knocked and rang the bell at the same time, causing the unlocked door to creep open and reveal a world that none of us could believe: half-naked hoochies . . . everywhere, all dancing up on somebody's man; and Melvin, Shae's boyfriend, was leading the way with a purple velvet cape around his neck. Looking exactly like Mr. Brown from the Tyler Perry plays.

He was doing the Souljah Boy in slow motion with two ghetto tricks to the DJ's mix of Souljah Girl. And when we looked, Josiah was doing the funky chicken. Tay looked at Seven. "Told you he wasn't no thug."

And as we walked in, it was as if the entire party went SCREATCH!!!!!!. Melvin stopped dancing instantly, slapping the girls he was dancing with in the face with the sides of his cape, knocking them to the floor.

"Bama ass," Shae snapped. "Nucka! I don't believe this," I could hear the tears in her throat. *"And I thought that was our dance!"*

"It is, Cornbread."

"Shut calling me Cornbread!"

"What you want me to call you, sexy toast?"

"Call me nothing!"

"Well, Nothing, it ain't even like that!"

"It don't even matter," Tay said as we all started taking off our earrings, "'cause it's so far on, that all y'all 'bout to know the meaning of off!"

"Seven, what are you doing?" Josiah asked as we started talking our stilettos off.

"I came—"

Seven was talking too slow, so Tay took over the argument. "We came to show you that she ain't the one!"

"You got this hoochie," I spat, "all in your grill and my sister at home crying?"

"Crying, for what?" Josiah looked confused.

"'Cause your playboy behind is trying to cheat," Tay snapped. "All 'cause she ain't give you no booty. Maybe she likes being a virgin."

"Could you stop talking so loud?" Seven blinked her eyes.

"What?" Josiah frowned. "I would never cheat on you. Didn't you get my text message?"

"Oh, here we go," Tay carried on, "every time a man knows he's wrong, all of a sudden he's sent a text message. Boy, please. Who you think gon' fall for that?"

Josiah looked at Seven. "You better go catch her. Now look at your phone!" he demanded while we all stood there, with the exception of Shae, who was still handling Melvin.

"I don't care!" Shae carried on. "You don't do the Souljah Boy in slow motion with nobody else!"

Seven looked at her phone and read her text messages. The first one was from Josiah.

"Baby, I made it over! Come celebrate your man's pledging Omega Psi Phi and bring your girls!"

"Oh . . ." she said off into a distance.

"Yeah, I know. Oh," Josiah snapped.

I squinted my eyes. "I swear to God I'ma puncha you in the face! Told you 'bout letting Tay hype you up!"

"Don't blame me!" Tay tried to say innocently.

"I was just sayin' . . . hey cutie." She waved to one of the guys across the room. "Don't I know you?"

"Ai'ight," Josiah gave Seven half a smile, "hit me wit' it."

She gave him the look, the one where her eyes glimmer sadness and her dimples sank in her cheeks.

"Don't even try it." He kissed her on the lips. "I'm listening."

"My fault." She whined, like a five year old.

"No," he gave Seven a sly smile. "I want to hear, 'I'm sorry.'"

"I'm sorry."

"Punk," I said under my breath and sucked my teeth so hard it's a wonder they stayed in my mouth. As soon as I got the opportunity, I was going to slap my sister in the head.

"Now give me a kiss," Josiah said and, of course, Seven melted. I felt like throwing up.

"So is this why you haven't called me?" floated over my shoulder. "'Cause you tryna be a sexy ass gangsta?" I turned around and it was Harlem. He handed me a styrofoam cup filled with soda. Instantly, my heart fluttered. "Are you stalking me?"

He laughed. "Don't flatter yourself. I go to school here. Josiah is my boy. We're both Q's."

"Aww." I did all I could to suppress my smile. "So what? Your chick has the day off?"

"Stop that." He grabbed me by the waist and started slow dancing with me, Lyfe Jennings' "Must Be Nice" was playing as we swayed from side to side. I placed my arms around his neck and he slid his hands in the back pockets of my capris. "Let me kick this to you real quick. I don't like girls with a whole buncha ra-ra and shootin' off at the mouth. If you got something to ask me, ask me, 'cause all that neck swingin' and lip poppin' you bringin' ain't even for you." He stroked my cheek and kissed me on the side of my neck. "Understand?"

I twisted my lips but I knew he could tell that I wanted to smile by my dimples sinking in my cheeks. "Please. Like you don't have a girl?"

"Was that a question?"

"Yes."

"Ai'ight, then ask me."

"Do you have a girl?"

"Nah. Why, you wanna be my girl?"

"Do you want me to be your girl?"

"Maybe . . . maybe that could be arranged."

"Yeah, right." I held my head down.

"Seriously," he lifted my chin.

"You don't have to flatter me." Me'Shell Ndegéocello's "Trust" was now playing and I felt like this was me and Harlem's song. It had been so long since I felt like this that I just felt like something had to be wrong. I mean, was he really feeling me or was I fooling myself again? God, I hated this. I placed my head against his chest and closed my eyes.

"Ole boy hurt you ma?" he whispered in my ear.

"Nah," I said, feeling tears beat against the back of my eyes, "not at all."

"Then why are you scared?"

"I'm not scared."

"You're not scared but your heart is racing against my chest."

I didn't respond.

"It's cool, ma. I'm not gon' hurt you."

For at least two more songs we swayed to the music and then I felt Harlem tilt his head down and press his lips against mine. At that very moment, as the possibility of love brushed against my feet, I decided to let myself go and I kissed him with all I had and even more . . .

By the time we got home, it was eight at night and I could smell my mother's cornbread from the front door.

"Where y'all been?" she asked us as Noah played with my brother on the floor.

"Uhmmmm," I said, "nowhere." I started to say at work, but being that neither one of us had our work uniforms on, that would've been an obvious lie.

"Yeah, okay." She arched one eyebrow and resumed reading her book. I couldn't believe she let the conversation go just like that. I wondered if I should check her for a fever.

"Fat Mama!" Cousin Shake yelled, walking into the living room, "and broke-down Lil' Kim, is that you? I been waitin' for you to come home all day!"

"Why?" I asked suspiciously. "And stop calling me broke-down Lil' Kim."

"'Just listen, 'cause," he tried to whisper, "I need you to help me respond to this li'l tender's message."

"Tender?" I frowned. "What are you talking about?"

"I'm exploring my options," he said.

"On what, Cousin Shake?" Seven asked.

"On MySpace. A li'l honey from around here saw my picture and wanted to hook up."

"And what about Melvin's mother?" I asked.

"Oh, I ain't tell you?"

"Tell us what?" Seven and I said simultaneously.

"We just friends. I told her I had a lotta playboy left in me and I needed to get out."

"I'ma throw up," Seven said, disgusted.

"Now come on," Cousin Shake walked over to the computer which sat in the dining room and logged onto his MySpace page. "I got about fifty-five messages already, I'm telling you, this li'l tender ready to get this poppin' and I am, too." He pulled up her profile.

"Oh my God," I gasped. "That's Ms. Minnie, Percy's mother."

"Uhmm, well, I likes me some Ms. Minnie." Cousin Shake growled.

"Yuck!"

"What you mean, yuck?" Cousin Shake asked. "You see that body on her? Shortie shaped—"

"Just like a hound dog," Seven cut him off.

"A hound dog?" Cousin Shake blinked in disbelief. "Keep it up and you coming off my top friend
list. Anyway," he pointed to the screen, "she said I
could ask her anything I wanted to, so I need y'all
help with what to ask."

"What you wanna know?" I asked him.

"First things first, since she only twenty-two—"

Seven started laughing. "More like seventy-
two."

"That's it," Cousin Shake snapped, clicking on
Seven's page. "Consider yourself blocked."

I could tell by the way Seven blinked she didn't
have a response for that.

"Now help me write this, Toi."

"Like I said, what you wanna know?"

"Does she live with her mama and does she
have a job?"

"Okay, well, ask her that."

He started typing, one finger at a time. "Do you
live in yo' mama's crib and is you on welfare?"

"You tryna talk about me, Cousin Shake?" I was
offended.

"No, baby, never."

"Ummm hmmm, what else you want to know?"

"Does she have any kids?"

"Well, type it." I pointed to the keyboard.

"How much," he typed, "baby daddy drama do
you have?"

"Wait a minute, Cousin Shake. You can't send
that—" and before I could tell him why, the phone
rang.

"I got it," I practically tripped over my feet answering it.

"Hello?" I said.

"Wassup ma?" It was Harlem. "I really enjoyed you today."

"I enjoyed you, too." I took the cordless phone and walked to my room.

"Oh, so that's how you gon' do me?" Cousin Shake yelled down the hall after me. "It's all good. I know y'all think I can't do this without you, but I can. I can read, you know. I'ma just send my love note the way it is. All I got to do is sign it," and I could hear him typing as he screamed, "Love Super Size Shake!'"

8

It was eleven at night and I was lying back on my bed with my feet propped against the wall, and I was basking in thoughts of Harlem. The only light coming into my room was from the moonlight, which snuck in between my mini blinds and left glowing stripes over half of my body. For once I let Noah sleep in his crib and the sound of his usual heavy breathing was blocked out by my thoughts and the slow jams on the radio.

The butterflies in my stomach fluttered in a thousand different directions as I wondered if I should call Harlem, or was our talking for hours on the phone last night enough for a few days. I mean, I didn't want him to think I was sweatin' him. But, I desperately wanted to hear his voice.

An hour later, into thinking about what I should do, my phone rang. I looked at the caller ID, and it was Harlem. "*Thank you, God.*" I smiled at the ceiling. I let it ring two more times and then answered, "Hello?"

"Wassup, beautiful?"

My heart skipped and the butterflies in my stomach flapped like they were in a race. "Who is this?" I said, as if I didn't know who it was.

He laughed. "Oh, you don't know my voice. So how many more dudes you have calling you?"

None. "Three."

"I hope that was a joke," he said seriously.

I laughed. "I was hoping you would call." *I hope I didn't give in too soon.* "I was just thinking about you."

"I was thinking about you too, ma. So what's good with you?"

"Nothing, just listening to music. Whatchu doing?"

"Getting ready to buy me Chinese food."

"Chinese is my favorite!" I said, a little too excited.

"What's your favorite dish?"

"Orange chicken and lo mein."

"Hold on for a minute." He clicked over and I wondered who could be calling him this time of the night. "Yeah." He clicked back over. "Let me hit you back in a minute."

Let him hit me back? Is that what he said? Yeah, yeah, I believe he did. I couldn't believe this! I knew it was only a matter of time before my bubble would bust.

Suddenly, I didn't wanna to hear anymore slow music, so I turned the radio off. To heck with love, like, lust, or whatever this nonsense that fluttered my in stomach was. Didn't I swear these feelings off anyway? So bump it! When my father left my mother and Qua did me dirty, I should've known that love had left the building. Yet here I was again. Jackass!

Before I could finish berating myself, my phone rang. "Yeah," I said with attitude. To heck with playing it off!

It was Harlem. "You got clothes on?"

"Excuse me?"

"Wait—" he laughed. "It's not what you think."

"Okay, because I was gon' say, you trying to be freaky?"

"It's all good ma. The phone wouldn't even do me justice."

Why was I imagining some nasty things? Okay, let me pull it back. "So, what does my clothes have to do with this conversation?"

"I wanted to make sure you were dressed. Come outside—I brought you some Chinese."

I couldn't stop blushing. I know he heard it in my voice. "You what?"

"I'm in front of your house. I brought you something to eat."

I couldn't believe this. I felt like he'd just asked to marry me. I looked down at what I had on, a pair of Victoria's Secret terry cloth shorts with PINK written across the booty and a matching tee shirt.

As I slipped on my pink flip-flops, I couldn't remember if I'd said goodbye when I hung up the phone.

I looked out the window to confirm he was still there and he was, looking as cute as he wanted to be in his '97 black, limited edition Jeep Cherokee. Before I went outside to meet him, I convinced Seven to watch Noah for me. When I opened my front door, I could see his smile. I walked over to his Jeep and got in. He had my food on the dashboard with a pair of chopsticks. Joe's "If I Was Your Man" was playing.

Instantly, I melted into the soft leather of his seat. I'd never been on a date like this. All Quamir ever did was take me to his house and leave me there while he went God knows where or took me to his boy's house, and left me with his girl like she was my friend or something. But something this sweet, nah, I'd never been treated like this before.

"I can't believe you did this for me." I bashfully covered my mouth.

"Why not?" he looked into my eyes. "I'm feelin' you."

"It's just that . . . that I never really had no guy be this sweet to me."

"Well, you never been my girl before, either. Stick with me, ma. There's more where this came from."

"You're special." I stroked his cheek and held his chin in my hand.

He blushed. "Nah, I'm just Harlem."

"Well, you're special to me."

"Really?" He moved his face in toward mine and we kissed. And as our tongues met, I realized this was the best kiss I'd ever had.

"Ai'ight." He broke our kiss and licked his bottom lip. My MAC lip glass had rubbed off my lips and was now gleaming on his. "Eat your food. Nothing's worse than cold Chinese."

"True." I laughed, and scooted over as close as I could to him.

"Come around to my side," he said, clicking the locks on the door.

I got out the car and walked to his side of the Jeep. He pushed his seat as far back as it would go, then lowered it to a reclining position. He nodded his head. "Sit right here."

I sat between his legs and snuggled against his chest. "How are you going to eat like this?" I asked him.

"Easy," he smiled, "you gon' feed me."

I melted even more. I took my chopsticks and shared my orange chicken and lo mein with him. "So, what's your major in college?" I asked him.

"Computer science."

"I like computers."

"Maybe when you go to college," he said, eating from my chopsticks, "you can major in computers and be like me."

"Yeah, picture that," I said, placing a piece of chicken in my mouth. "Nah, I was thinking about

X-ray technician or something that doesn't take so long."

"You should go to college, ma." I gave him a sip of the soda he brought for me. "There's no experience like it."

"When I was younger, I always wanted to go to Spelman," I confessed. "Actually me, my sister, and our best friends made a pact to go."

"So what did you want to major in?"

"English, I wanted to be a teacher."

"You should be a teacher and you should go to Spelman," he said, eating another bite. "Atlanta is the bomb. That's where my mom's moving. I thought about transferring to Clark or Morehouse when she goes."

"Why?" I playfully whined. "You gon' miss your mommy?"

"Yeah," he said, "I will. My dad died earlier this year, my sister is getting married in a week, and her fiancé is from here, so she's not going anywhere. And I just hate to see my mother in Atlanta alone."

"Oh, I'm sorry to hear that. About your dad, that is."

"It's cool. But I'm saying, I think you should go Spelman or at least think about it."

"Well, you never know what the future holds." I placed the chopsticks in the empty carton and leaned back against his chest.

He ran his fingers through my hair and before I knew it, we'd talked about everything, from our

Ni-Ni Simone

first kiss to our first trip in first grade. I shared things with him, I'd never shared with another living soul. And no matter how far-fetched they felt to me, he made me feel like maybe I could do more than dream. Maybe I could achieve.

I even told him about Quamir, without ever mentioning that I had a son and Quamir was my son's father. Harlem told me about an ex-girlfriend who'd broken his heart, someone he'd cared deeply about. This was the best date I'd ever been on in my life and before I knew it, we'd both fallen asleep. We were awakened by the dawning sun smiling upon us.

"Harlem," I called, and he slowly peeled his eyes open. "I have to go in the house. My mother will be home from work soon."

"Wow," he yawned, "it's morning. I hope you still respect me," he joked.

"Shut up." I playfully balled up my fist and he placed me in a pretend headlock.

"Alright, alright." I laughed.

"Look ma, this was ai'ight," he released me from the headlock. "I like chillin' with you. Maybe we can do this again?"

"Maybe." I kissed him. "Maybe."

We said goodnight or rather good morning and then I stood on the side walk and watched him leave. As I walked on the porch, I saw Cousin Shake parking his tricked-out hearse across the street. His clothes were disheveled and the reason why we called him Cousin Shake revealed itself before my eyes. "Cousin Shake," I said, concerned because I'd never seen him like this before. "What's

wrong? Why are you looking like that?"

"You can't handle it, broke-down Lil' Kim," he spoke haltingly. Suddenly, I was nervous. I mean, he got on my nerves but I didn't want anything to happen to him.

"What?" I said in a panic. "Tell me. I can handle anything."

"Well," he cleared his throat, "I met that li'l honey from the computer."

"Percy's mama? And?"

"And," he smiled, "Your Cousin Shake . . . just finished gettin' some of Ms. Minnie's fifty-year-old booty."

"Oh . . . my . . . God!!!!!!!!!"

9

"Man-Man!" I pounded on the wall. "What is all that bangin'?"

"Shut up!" he yelled back. "I'm tryna get my Kool-Aid hustle on and you disturbing me!"

"You brother is the worst!" I rolled my eyes at Seven as I placed Noah beside me on the bedroom floor so he could play with his toys.

"Would y'all come on," Tay leaned forward on both elbows.

"Please," Shae said as she lay on her back. "Truth, dare, consequences, private, or repeat?"

"It's your turn, Seven," Tay said.

"No, it's not," Seven said. "I just went, now it's your turn to go, and I asked you the question."

"Okay, I want truth."

"So," Seven smiled, "I been wantin' to ask you

this for a while—is it true that you gave Shim-
daddy some woo-woo?"

"What the hell is woo-woo?" Tay laughed.

"Some booty, girl."

"No," Tay said, defensively. "I just got on my
knees and kissed him."

"Ill." I frowned. "No wonder they keep following us around."

"Shut up. I felt sorry for him. He said he never
had a kiss before. Plus, he paid me fifty dollars to
do it."

"So, you're a kissing whore now?" I laughed.

"Whatever. All I know is he had the money."
She cracked up.

"You're stupid!" Shae cracked up.

"Okay." Tay sat up and looked at me. "Truth,
dare, consequences, private or repeat?"

"Truth." I smiled. For the most part, we always
picked truth.

"Is Harlem the best boyfriend you ever had?"

That was easy. "Yes."

"Okay." Seven bit her bottom lip. "Since that
was easy, I wanna ask you another one."

"Go ahead." I handed Noah a stuffed animal.

"What does Harlem think of you having a baby?"

I paused, "He hasn't asked me if I have a baby."

"He shouldn't have to." Shae frowned. "You
should just tell him."

"I am. I just haven't done it yet."

"You embarrassed?" Tay asked.

"No."

"Well, if you don't hurry up," Seven interjected, "he's going to think you lied to him."

"No he won't."

"Yes he will."

"Well, then I'll just have to deal with that. Why are you asking me that, anyway?"

"Because Josiah told me that he really likes you and he was wondering if Harlem knew you had a baby."

"So! What? Having a baby is like having the plague?"

"No," Seven snapped. "He said he just didn't wanna be telling your business."

"Uhmm hmm, well, tell him thank you."

"Oops, no you didn't." Shae rolled her neck. "Anyway, it's my turn," Seven said.

I looked at Shae. "Truth, dare, consequences, private or repeat?"

"Dare."

"Okay, I dare you to tell one of your best friend's secrets. We already know Seven's a virgin, so not that."

Shae looked at Seven and then back at us. "She's not a virgin anymore."

"Oh no you didn't tell my business!" Seven screamed, providing the confirmation we needed to know that this was true.

"They asked," Shae snapped back.

"You could've lied."

"You know whomever gets caught lying has to pay twenty dollars! Not."

"Whatever!" Seven was pissed and I couldn't believe this.

"I hope she's lying!" I looked at Seven.

"No, she's not." Seven playfully balled up her fist and pointed it at Shae.

"Oh . . . my . . . goodness," Tay said. "Don't hold nothin' back. I want to hear it all."

"I don't believe this." I had an attitude. "But go on, what happened?"

"A few nights ago, we were kissing . . . and he was feeling on me. And it felt comfortable, like it was something I wanted to do, so I did."

"Did it hurt?" Tay asked.

"Yeah, but he was gentle."

"Forget all that," I said. "Did you use a condom?'"

"Magnum extra large." She laughed and shot Shae and Tay high fives.

"You still shouldn't have done it. You should've waited," I said.

"Why? You didn't."

"You just should've waited, 'cause sometimes after you have sex, things change."

"Like what?"

"They stop sweatin' you." Before I could go on, the phone rang. I looked at the caller ID. "It's Harlem," I whispered.

"I thought you said he was getting ready for his sister's wedding?" Seven asked.

"That's what he told me," I said as I picked up the phone. "Hello?"

"Yo, Pretty Girl," he said, and I could hear frustration in his voice. "Can you tie a tie?"

"Yeah. Why?"

"'Cause I can't get this."

"What, a tie?"

"Yeah."

"Yeah, I can tie a tie. My daddy taught me."

"Cool, then come outside and tie this for me. I'm turning the corner now."

"Okay." And I hung up.

I looked at Seven. "That's the result of me not giving him no booty. He's coming over here for me to tie his tie."

"Whoooo! Somebody ring the alarm!"

"Don't hate," I said, leaving them on the floor playing the game. "Don't hate."

"Where are you going?" Tay asked.

"Outside to tie my baby's tie."

"Perfect timing. What better time than now to introduce him to his step-son?"

"Don't play. I'm not taking Noah out there like that. Plus, he's in a rush."

"Uhmm hmmm," they looked at me suspiciously.

I didn't have time to acknowledge them, so I didn't. I walked outside and the evening breeze was cool. Harlem leaned against the hood of his Jeep with a loose tie around his neck. He was dressed in a two-piece suit looking as fine as he wanted to be. I walked up to him and he slid his hands in my back pocket as I fixed his tie. Fantasia's "When I See You" was playing on the car radio. It floated out the window and into the street.

"You know," he said, as I tied his tie, "this song reminds me of you."

"Really?" I said, as we started to sway to the music.

"Yeah, it does."

"And why is that?" I straightened his collar and admired my handiwork.

"Shhh," he said as I slid my hands around his neck and locked my fingers, "just listen to the words."

I did. I closed my eyes and we swayed until the song was over. I couldn't believe I was slow dancing in the middle of South 14th Street, but I didn't care, I wanted to be here forever. And when the song was over, I hated that it had to end. "Yo, I need to go," he whispered in my hair.

"I know," I said.

"I'ma see you soon?"

"You know it ma."

"Alright."

"Oh," he pressed his lips against mine, "and don't tell nobody I was in the middle of the hood, dancing in the street." He winked, jumped in his Jeep and left. When I got in the house, I fell against the door and Seven, Tay, and Shae were standing there. "And you ain't giving up no booty?" they all said simultaneously. "Okay."

10

I think I'm in love or caught up. True story—no lie. It's like every day I feel like I'm getting a new pair of Gucci shoes. And for the first time, I love being seventeen; there's only one thing. I have to tell Harlem that I have a son. Which I don't know how to do.

Most dudes around here just ask if you have a baby, but Harlem hasn't, not even once. He hasn't even hinted at it, and every time I go out with him, I feel guilty, like I'm living a lie. And it's not that I don't love my son, because I do. It's just that . . . honestly, and keepin' it real, I'ma little embarrassed to say I'm a teenage mom. And yeah, it's mad chicks around here with babies and it's not like I'm ashamed of my baby. I'm ashamed of my situation.

Believe me, guys are the worst when they find

out you have a baby. And no matter how many babies they have, they always think that if you have a baby, you must be stupid, or easy, or they look at you like you have a whole lotta drama, and before you know it, you've gone from being wifey to being the jump-off. And that's not what I want. But I have to tell Harlem about my son . . . and if he trips, then I'll cut him off. Yeah, that's it. If he trips, it's a wrap.

As usual, when Harlem comes to pick me up, I run outside so he won't ask to come in. "Why are you always running out to meet me? You don't want me in your house or something?" he asked.

"No," I lied. "It's not even like that." Why didn't I just tell the truth? As we pulled off, I noticed how the kids were lined up around the corner for Man-Man's Kool-Aid stand.

"Yo, your brother be killin' it."

"I know. And it's just Kool-Aid."

"I hope so." Harlem laughed. "He ain't selling no gin and juice, is he?"

"Boy, please. He is only ten."

"Ai'ight . . . so . . . you missed me?"

"Of course," I said, looking out the window. It was ten o'clock in the morning and it was already sweltering hot. I wanted to tell him about Noah right then and there, but I figured I'd wait until we were on our way back.

"Toi," Harlem called me.

"Yeah."

"When is your prom?"

"My prom?"

"Yeah, when is it?"

"Well, we decided when we were juniors that it would be May 20. Why?"

"Because in case I transfer to Georgia, of course assuming I am your date, I'll know when to fly back up."

"You would fly all the way back up here for my prom?"

"Yeah."

I didn't even know what to say to that. This had to be a dream.

Of course, Great Adventure was filled with a sea of people everywhere and the lines were crazy long. "I used to love coming here when I was a kid," I said as we walked hand and hand, trying to decide what we were going to ride.

"Yeah?" he placed his arm over my right shoulder and tossed it around my neck. I laid my head against his chest. "I used to love it here. Yo, you ever ride Free Fall?" he asked.

"Free Fall?" I stopped dead in my tracks.

"What, you a punk?"

"I'm not no punk."

"Well, let's see."

We stood in line for twenty minutes to ride the Free Fall and of course I was scared. But I wasn't going to let him know that. These types of rides weren't my thing, but whatever. I got on, buckled myself in as Harlem sat beside me. As the ride started, I grabbed his hand and closed my eyes. The car climbed a thousand feet in the sky—well, not really but it felt like it—and then, without warning, the ride dropped us at like sixty miles an hour and popped us back up like a rubber band. I squeezed my eyes so tight they hurt. I am never doing this again!

Once the ride was over, I tried to play off how bad my legs were shaking by running behind Harlem and playfully jumping on his back like a five-year-old kid.

"Awww," he said, "my baby was scared?" He hooked his arms behind my knees.

"No!"

"Toi, you were screaming in my ear."

"Ok, maybe I was a little scared, but not much," I said as my legs swung at his side.

"Uhmm hmm. Ai'ight, so let's go on the loopy loop."

"Uhmm, let's not. I want a prize."

"You want your man to win you something?" he asked. "Ai'ight, I got you." I slid off his back and we went to the basketball game. I knew for sure we would win. After all, he was six-foot-two.

A few minutes later, the game was over.

"How you gon' lose the game?" I didn't know whether to have an attitude or laugh.

"That mess is rigged. You saw those balls going in the basket."

"No," I laughed. "I saw them hit the rim and come out the basket."

"Whatever," he said as we stopped by the "Shooting Water in a Balloon Until It Pops" game.

"I don't need you to win me a prize. I'll do it," I said as Harlem laid two dollars on the table. I positioned myself behind a pink water gun.

"Girl, you can't beat me on this." Harlem took position behind a black water gun.

"I can show you better than I can tell you." We didn't even pay attention to the other people playing because we just knew we were going to win. That is, until a little kid started screaming because his balloon popped while mine and Harlem's was still rising. Oh, I wanted to cop this little dude in the face.

"Yo," Harlem laughed, "did you see that dude? He was like a super kid."

"Uhmm hmm, and this is the second time you lost. I'ma start looking at you sideways."

"Shut up." He laughed as we moved on to the next game and I'm not sure what happened but suddenly Harlem started killing it. I was like "damn look at my man." As a matter of fact, he even went back to the basketball and water balloon game and redeemed himself. I had so many stuffed animals that it was crazy. It was official; this was the best date I'd ever had in my life.

We headed to the parking lot, exhausted. "Harlem," I smiled. "I really like you, and you are real special to me."

"That's sweet, baby. I feel the same way."

"And we've been really kickin' it and everything."

"So where's all this coming from? You tryna break up with me?"

"No!" I shook my head. "Silly. But look, let me ask you this."

"What?"

"Are there any type of girls that you wouldn't date?"

"Yeah," he said quickly. "Short ones. I'm too big for a short chick."

"That's it, short chicks. And you would date any other kind of girl?"

"Yeah, I guess. I mean, if I don't like her, I just wouldn't kick it to her."

Okay, since he doesn't discriminate, maybe this is the perfect time to tell him that I have a baby. I couldn't help but smile as I started to daydream about us being a family. Noah's car seat in the back of Harlem's Jeep and the three of us just chillin' forever.

". . . and teenage mothers," he said, seemingly out of nowhere.

I looked at him. "What?" I was so busy day-dreaming that I had tuned him out.

"Teenage mothers," he repeated. "I can't stand chicks with kids. Most of the time they're stupid, with no goals, and easy. That's why the kid doesn't do statistics."

"Statistics?" I couldn't believe he said that.

"Statistics," he repeated. "They're too much baggage and drama. I'm just nineteen. What I look like with a ready-made family? Please. I'm good.

I'm not tryna give no babies, so I ain't tryna get none. 'Specially no baby that's not mine."

He didn't know it, but I felt like he'd spat on me at least three times. I swallowed and sniffed. "Ai'ight," I said, pushing my bruised feelings to the side.

"So, what you wanna do now?" he asked.

"Go home," I said as the sun started to set. "I'ma little tired anyway."

"Ai'ight," he said as we started walking toward his car.

"Toi."

"Yeah?"

"We got a long ride ahead," he said, "so don't be up in the car falling asleep and dreaming."

"Harlem, please." I frowned, "Believe me, I'm learning not to dream."

11

It was eleven o'clock at night. I'd just laid Noah down, Keyshia Cole's "Let It Go" was on the radio. I'd been avoiding Harlem's phone calls for a week and it was making me sick to my stomach. I was missing him like crazy, but I couldn't deny my son . . . any more.

In between listening to the radio, my sister was talking to me about Spelman and how we needed to apply there. I barely paid her any attention—with the way things were going, who saw me doing anything else other than being somebody's mama and struggling to live my life. At least that's what I felt reduced to . . . or is reduced the right word? My son was the most important person in the world to me and if I didn't love him, I wouldn't be profiling at IHOP, believe me, but college, paleeze. Spelman was just another one of those dreams I would have to live without.

"Seven, could you . . . talk about something else?" Though Noah had just fallen asleep, I turned the radio up—this was my jam—matter of fact—this was everybody's jam.

Seven tooted her lips. It's funny how we were twins but looked totally different. Nothing but our dimples and black hair were the same.

"Toi," she said, pointing to the college applications she had spread on my bed. "We need to apply now."

"Seven, newsflash, I'm not going to college. And if I do, I'ma be in Essex County all my life, taking one class at a time . . . forever." I flipped through the current issue of *Vibe Vixen* and flopped down on the futon on the other side of the room, while Seven sat Indian style on my bed and looked at me like I was crazy.

"Are you retarded?" she spat. "Who told you that garbage? I know mommy is hard on you, but dang, she never said roll over and die."

"Excuse you," I flipped the page. "I didn't think going to Essex County was rolling over and dying."

"I'm not talking about that. There's nothing wrong with Essex County. You're the problem, acting like you have no hope. Ill, what is that?"

"Seven, have you been asleep? I no longer have a life. The only time I party is when I go to IHOP. How whack is that?" I was resentful when I said that, but that's how I felt. "I don't go anywhere, my friends have their own lives, and the only reason why you're home so much is because Josiah is at school—"

"Did I tell you my boo is a good look for the NBA?"

"What?" I was excited.

"Yes, he entered the draft and he's a hot lottery pick. So, it's a sure shot."

"So when you two getting married?"

"Girl, please," she frowned at me, "he gon' wait until I get outta college. I have to set me up first."

"Excuse me, you would be, just by being his girl."

"Forget being his girl. I gotta be my own girl first and then we can talk about marriage. I don't know about you, but I'm depending on me to get what I need to succeed in life."

"True."

"I know it is, anyway," Seven said. "Wassup with Harlem?"

"It's over." I snapped.

"Why?"

"It just is."

"Broke down!" Cousin Shake yelled. "Get the door. It's probably my tender coming to get some'a Cousin Shake's honey, but I'm in the bathroom. Tell her to go in my room, light the incense, and put the best of Run DMC on. Tell her Big Daddy will be there in a minute."

"Yuck." I twisted my mouth as I walked toward

the door. Before I opened the door, I asked, "Who is it?"

"Quamir."

"What?" What was he doing here?

"What do you want?" I asked through the door.

"I came to see my son."

Now that pissed me off. I snatched the door open. "You for real or you just want me to go off?"

"Oh, I can't see my son now?"

"You haven't seen him but twice in his life. Now, all of a sudden you coming to see him at almost midnight. Boy, please." I rolled my eyes to the sky. "Do I look crazy?"

"Oh, it's like that Toi?"

"Pretty much. Plus, my mother'll be here any minute from work and if she sees you here, she gon' bug. So just go."

"Oh, so now your mother is more important than me?"

I blinked my eyes. "What?"

"Toi," my mother snapped as she pressed onto the porch. "What is this?"

See, this is exactly what I didn't want. "It's not what it look like, ma."

"I told you, I didn't want him at my house. He can't take care of this baby, he can't come through my door."

"Yo," Quamir frowned at my mother, "you better go 'head. I'm not no kid."

"Don't be talking to my mother like that, Quamir," I snapped. "You better calm down."

"Oh, now you flexin'?" Quamir was beyond pissed. "Remember this when you calling me beggin'."

"Boy, I ain't called you in so long. Please."

"If you don't leave my damn house right now," my mother stepped into his face, "I will call the police on you!"

"This how you gon' do me, Toi?" Before I could respond, he said, "You know we really through, right? Since you gon' let somebody disrespect me," he looked my mother up and down, "I'm going to be with Shanice!" He stepped off the porch.

"Do I look concerned?" I yelled behind him. "Go be with her—matter of fact, what's taking you so long to get there? And if you get in my mother's face again, we gon' see if you live to get to Shanice!" And I slammed the door.

"Ma, it wasn't what you thought."

"It never is, Toi! You just keep making one mistake after the next. As soon as I think you're getting better, you just seem to get worse!" She stormed into her bedroom and slammed the door.

A few minutes later, I knocked. "What?" she snapped.

"Can I come in?"

"Yes."

I pushed the door open and I could still see the disgust on her face. "Ma, do you hate me?"

My mother looked completely confused and if I wasn't mistaken, she even looked like her feelings were hurt. "Hate you? Do you think I hate you?"

"How come you always go off on me? You never listen to me! Like you just go off at the drop of a dime."

"I don't always go off on you," she said, more as a question than a statement.

"Yes you do, like tonight with Quamir. That wasn't my fault but you snapped on me."

"I just get so frustrated, Toi." She patted the bed for me to come sit next to her. "Let me tell you something. I love you. I love you so much that it hurts me to see you making mistakes that I know are going to cost you. I'll admit, I'm disappointed. And maybe I am going about it the wrong way and being a little too hard."

"Ya think?"

"Toi," she gave me half a smile, "I had you and your sister at nineteen so I know what it's like to be a young mother. I just want so much more for you."

"Ma," I looked at her, "don't you think I'm disappointed too? Don't you think I hurt? I mean, look at me." I held my fingers out as if I was counting on them. "I'm on welfare, I can't go out with my friends anymore—matter of fact, they don't even invite me out. Quamir is exactly what everyone said he would be. Sometimes I feel like I'ma go crazy because I'm so confused. Like, it is so not cute being in this situation. Sometimes I wonder if I hate my own self." Tears streamed down my cheeks.

My mother took my hands into hers. "Let me

tell you something. Before your father and I got married, I was on welfare."

"You were?" I couldn't believe it. "Daddy didn't help you out?"

"Yes, he did. He's always taken care of you, but we were both young and high-strung. But we had two beautiful babies and we had to do what we had to do. So I accepted welfare. I took my mother's advice—she said that she'd paid taxes long enough for me not to be ashamed of needing some help."

"How long were you on welfare?"

"Two years, and then your father and I got married. Even though I never liked the idea of having to get food stamps, Medicaid, and whatever little money they gave me, taking care of you became more important than pride. What I learned is that there was nothing to be embarrassed of because being on welfare was the means to something better. It wasn't forever, and now I have my own house, I work two jobs but I have money in the bank, a car, and I have all the other things that I've wanted in life and what I don't have I'll work on it and eventually I'll get it."

I sat and stared at my mother for a moment. For the first time since I became a teenage mom, I had hope and I could see myself actually being something—somebody. "Ma, you know what I've always wanted to be when I grew up?"

"What, a pink Power Ranger?"

"Ma," I laughed. "I told you that when I was seven."

"I know and I told you—you could be whatever you want to be."

I fell out laughing. "Well, it's not a pink Power Ranger." 101

"So what is it and don't say the red one."

"Ma, be serious."

"I'm listening."

"A teacher."

Her face lit up with delight. "A teacher?"

"Yeah." I gave her a prideful smile. "I like English. So I would like to be a high school English teacher."

"And that," she said, "would make me the proudest mother alive!"

"I love you ma." I hugged her tight, like I used to when I was a little girl.

"I love you too li'l mama," she said, calling by the nickname she gave me as a child. "Now," she said, "go to bed."

12

It had been a week now. Quamir kept stalking me and Harlem kept calling. I didn't know how or when this happened, but life as I knew it had been shut down. Even if I wanted to go out with Harlem, I couldn't. I couldn't find a babysitter to save my life.

I kept lying to Harlem and I knew he knew that something was up. This was the longest time I'd gone without seeing him since we first started kickin' it. And I knew I should just tell him I have a son, but it was so much easier to just let it all go . . . or at least I thought it was.

"What you thinkin' about, girl?" Tay said as she collected the tip off her table.

"Harlem." I frowned. "I've been avoiding him."

"Why you dissin' your boo?"

"Somebody say boo? 'Cause have no fear, Percy, Cle'otis, and Shim-daddy is here!"

"I wish I had some Raid," I squinted my eyes, "because I'd spray yo' ass."

He curled the corner of his top lip. "And I still wouldn't die, girl." He snapped his mouth at me like a dog.

I shuddered. I swear I wanted to Mace 'em. Percy and his crew were all dressed in double-breasted sky blue tuxedos with white ruffled shirts. "You thinkin' 'bout me?" Percy growled. "Just say it, homie."

"Why don't you fly away!" Tay snapped at Percy.

"Why don't you give me a li'l, jump-off!"

"Who you calling a jump-off Lil' Bootsy?" Percy's mother screamed as she stormed out of the bathroom.

"Dang," Percy whined. "Mamaaaaaaaaa."

"Don't mama me. Y'awl lookin' like a loose pack of flies, following these girls around!" She grabbed him by the ear while mushing Cle'otis and Shim-daddy in the head. "I'm so tired of you messing up your church clothes."

"Mama—" Percy cut his mother off.

"I'm talkin'—"

"Mama—"

"Oh, you cuttin' me off?" She pinched his ear even harder. "Where ya manners at Lil' Bootsy? This is yo' problem, ya mouth. Seems your mouth bigger than yo' body. That's why you going to church tonight, so you can pray and ask God to teach you how to break yo'self, fool. Now get on back to the table."

If I weren't so heartbroken I would laugh.

"I'm concerned," Tay said.

"About who, Percy? I think he was dropped as a baby," I said, answering my own question.

"Forget Percy. We all know he's crazy. I'm concerned about you. Why you playin' Harlem? I don't understand. I thought you liked him."

"I do."

"So why you tossing him to the left?"

"Okay, listen," I said as we walked toward the kitchen to pick up our customers' food. "He told me he doesn't date teenage mothers."

"For real?" She looked surprised. "Even after you told him you had a baby. You did tell him, right?"

"Wrong."

"You trippin'," she shook her head, "real hard."

"You don't understand. He said he doesn't do 'statistics,' and he said I had too much drama and a whole buncha ra-ra."

"He said that about you personally?"

"Well, no. He just said teen moms—"

"You're crazy. You owe him an explanation."

"Uhmm, maybe."

"Ladies," my manager said, clearing his throat, "your customers are waiting."

"Call him." Tay said as we parted.

She had a point. Maybe I should tell him. After all, it had been two weeks and I'm sure he suspected something. After I sat my customers' food on the table, and collected my tip from another table, I stepped to the back so I could use my phone. As I went to flip it open, I heard someone saying, "Hello?"

"Toi." It was my mother.

"Yes."

"What do you think about us giving Cousin Shake a birthday party?"

"If you want."

"I mean something small. You can invite some of your friends, Josiah, *Harlem . . .*" she said with emphasis.

"Harlem? How do you know Harlem?"

"Because he was by here today."

"He was?" I said in disbelief.

"Uhmm hmm, he came inside and everything." My heart skipped a beat. "He saw Noah?"

"No, Noah was asleep, but he was looking for you and he asked me to have you please call him."

"I'm not calling him."

"Why? He's cute and he's in college. I'm impressed."

"You don't understand, ma."

"Toi—would you be seventeen, sometimes. Goodness." Now I was confused—one minute I'm too immature and the next I'm too grown—see, I can't win. "Loosen up," she continued.

"I can't believe you, ma."

"Look, I'll babysit, but call him. Go out and have a good time."

"Okay." I smiled.

I only had a second before my manager would be looking for me, so I called him quickly. I got straight to the point. "I wanna see you."

"When, last week?" he snapped.

"Funny. And I can't talk long, so pick me up around six."

"Ai'ight ma, whatever."

"You coming?"

He stalled. "Yeah, I'll be there."

My heart fluttered for the rest of my shift. I couldn't wait to see him, and I was determined to be honest. Just spit it out. I'll hold my diaphragm in and say, "Harlem, I have a baby. A son. That's right, and if you don't like it, then get ta steppin'!" Yeah, that's it. That's exactly it.

I sucked my teeth. I was sounding so damn dumb!

"I know you don't think you should go on a date when you have a sick baby at home."

I wanted so bad to say why not? I couldn't believe this. Noah was fine when I left home this morning and now he's running a fever. Jesus. "No ma," I hesitated, "I know I should stay home." I wanted to scream and just lose it, but what good would it do?

"Okay, I'm just checking." She held Noah in her

arms and I placed the dropper of Tylenol in his mouth. "'Cause mothers should be home when they have sick children. Just tell boyfriend he'll have to come another night. I mean, Harlem seems like a nice guy. I'm sure he'll understand." Noah started to cry and she placed him on her shoulder.

I placed the Tylenol back in the refrigerator. "I have to go to the bathroom." Once I walked in the bathroom, I flipped my cell open and called Harlem.

"Harlem?"

"Wassup? I was just about to come through."

"Listen," I sighed. "I'm not gon' be able to go."

"What?" I could tell he was put off. "Something happened?"

"No."

"No? So you call and say you're not going and nothing happened? What's up with you? You seeing somebody else?"

"I can barely see you. Now you think I'm seeing somebody else too?"

"I don't know, you tell me. Know what ma," he said, sounding distant. "It's cool. I'm not gon' go through this with you."

"Go through what?"

"Nothing," he said. "Nothing."

"So what you saying?"

"I'm saying, I'm out," and he hung up.

Tears welled in my eyes and I started to cry. All my lessons in life, I learned the hard way. It's like this was so simple yet so hard to do at the same time. As I wiped my eyes and came out of the bathroom, my mother yelled, "Toi, Seven, I'm going to pick something up from my job and I'll be right back. Noah's in his crib and Toi, remember to check on him. If his fever feels worse, you call me."

"Okay." I went in my room and closed the door. As I grabbed the remote to turn on the television, there was a knock on my window, shaking the glass. I walked over and pulled the curtain back. It was Quamir. "Open the door!"

After I came out of momentary shock, I looked at him like he was crazy. "Lose yourself."

"Please."

I sucked my teeth. "Go to the front door!" I walked down the short hallway and snatched the door open. "What do you want?" I snapped. "My mother told you not to come back here!"

"Look." He grabbed my hand and I snatched it back. "I just came to apologize and see if we can get this back on track."

"What?" Was he on drugs? "Are you high?"

"High off you."

"Toi!" Seven called me as she walked into the living room from the back, "Noah was crying," she said, slowly noticing Quamir standing at the door, "and I was going to give him a bottle but there's no more milk."

"I'll buy it," Quamir volunteered.

"What?" Seven and I said simultaneously.

"I said I'll buy it. He's my son and from now on out I'm going to be here for him."

I must be dreaming. "Are you serious?"

"Yes," he looked at me, "I am."

"I'll watch him until you come back." Seven volunteered. "Better go 'head and get that milk before the other baby mama be calling."

I squinted my eyes at Seven, and then I looked at Quamir. "Okay." I grabbed my purse, "and he needs some Pampers, too."

"I got you." Quamir smiled.

As we rode to Walgreens, I wondered what was on Quamir's mind that he was back in my face. Last I checked, he hated me and now he was trying to be nice? Huh? "So Toi," he said, "I really would like for us to be a family again."

"Boy, please." I sucked my teeth.

"Boy please, what?" he said as we pulled into the parking lot. "I know that I haven't done everything that I needed to do, but I really wanna be with you."

Whatever. When we walked into the store, I headed down the baby aisle for formula, and Quamir picked up a pack of Trojans, and then he headed toward the snack aisle. "What hoochie you buying all that stuff for?" I asked after I'd gotten what I needed.

"Why you so interested?" he smiled at me. "I'm giving you the opportunity to do something about all those other *hoochies*."

I fell out laughing. I was cracking up so hard that I didn't even notice the water on the floor, and before I knew anything, I was falling. Quamir caught me.

"Thank you." I said, noticing how he was holding me a little too closely.

"You smell so good." He buried his nose in my neck and as I went to push him off, I looked up and Harlem was standing there. He didn't crack even the slightest smile. "You wanna introduce me to your friend?" he said, looking at Quamir.

"Oh," I paused, breaking Quamir's embrace. "This is Quamir." I could tell Harlem's feelings were hurt.

"Wassup?" Quamir held me around the waist.

"What are you doing?" I snapped at Quamir. "Get off of me!" I turned back toward Harlem and as quickly as he came, he'd left. My heart sank to the bottom of my chest. "Damn!"

"You know what, Toi? I'm sick of you playing me!" Quamir spat.

"Playing you?"

"You think I'ma keep sweatin' you. Well, hell no. You're wrong. Buy your own milk, Pampers and shit."

"What?" I couldn't believe this. "Was this a set up?"

"Call it whatever, but I'm not chasing you no more!"

"Fine, I'll pay for my son's stuff, just drop me

off and go back to the section of hell you flew out of off."

"Better catch yo' ass a bus." And he left.

I couldn't believe this . . . I absolutely . . . could . . . not believe this. I didn't even get mad, I paid for my son's stuff and walked home.

Once I got home, and made sure my son was okay, then picked up the phone and called Harlem. The call went straight to voicemail and I hung up.

"What took you so long?" Seven asked as I walked into my bedroom door.

"Girl, you not gon' believe this." I shook my head and tears came to my eyes.

"Did Quamir try something with you?"

I cried and told her everything that had happened. By the time I was through, I was a babbling mess.

"Go lay down," she said, "I'll look after Noah."

"Alright." I wiped my eyes. "Alright."

13

"Amir!" My mother yelled as I walked into the living room to meet Tay, who sat waiting for me on the porch. "Why are all these kids lined up here at ten o'clock in the morning? What do they want?"

"Kool-Aid," he said, cheesin'.

"Didn't I tell you to stop selling that Kool-Aid? I had to cuss out Margarite down the street because she said you were selling Alizé and not Kool-Aid."

"Ma," he put on a smile that was simply a little too innocent. "I would never do anything like that."

"You better not." She grabbed her purse for work, "'cause you know I will bust dat ass."

"Bye ma." He smiled as she walked to the door. "Yeah, I know. Bye."

"Hi, Mrs. McKnight," Tay said as my mother walked down the stairs.

"Hi. Toi, listen out for Noah. He's asleep. Seven's inside but she'll be leaving for work soon."

"Okay, ma. Bye."

"Love you."

"Okay, girl." Tay said, sitting on the porch with me, "What happened with Quamir the other night?"

"How you know about Quamir?" I asked her, surprised.

"Ronnique told me."

"Ronnique?"

"Yeah. Ronnique found out from Deeyah, who found out from Shanice, who said that Quamir told her. Ronnique said that you been stalking Quamir, calling him every day."

"What?"

"Don't worry, I set Ronnique straight and then I told her to carry that back."

"Girl, it was nothing," I just didn't feel like recapping the whole thing, "other than Quamir being Quamir."

"That bad?"

I shook my head. "Even worse." I gave her the Cliff note version of what Quamir had done.

"He get the award for crazy-azz of the year."

"Exactly."

"Well, on to better things. We need to start filling out our applications so we can be ready for Spelman."

I rolled my eyes to the sky. "I don't know about Spelman anymore."

"And why not?"

"News flash. I have a baby."

"I thought your mother wanted to move to Atlanta."

"She mentioned it once, last year some time, but I haven't heard anything since."

"Well, you better push up," Tay said. "I mean, do all your dreams have to die because you had a baby? Dang."

Before I could answer her question, Harlem pulled up and parked his Jeep in front of my house. I was surprised to see him and I could tell by the look on his face that he had something on his mind he had to say.

"Okay," I looked at Tay. "I'ma catch you later."

"Do that," Tay said, "maybe we can go to the mall or something."

She waved at Harlem as he stepped up on the bottom step of the porch and leaned against the railing. "Wassup with you?" he looked me in the face. "And don't lie, you been lying enough."

"I don't know." I hunched my shoulders.

"Lie number one. You only got one more chance and I'ma officially bounce. I don't sweat chicks and I don't chase 'em, but you got me running all over the place. And I ain't feeling that. I'ma man, ma. You ever had a man before or you too busy running around with boys who leave you in the store."

I blinked in disbelief. "How do you know he left me in the store?"

"Because I watched you walk home."

"You followed me?" I closed one eye and play-fully said, "You stalking me, Harlem?"

"Do I look like I'm playing with you?"

"No."

"I followed you to be sure you were safe. You only lived around the corner, otherwise I would've given you a ride. But don't try and change the subject. Wassup with you?"

"Harlem—"

"You gon' tell me?"

"Harlem?"

"You back with ole boy?"

"Let me explain."

"Know what—cancel the explanation. It's a wrap. I can't believe I was feeling you like that. And Josiah gon' tell me to talk to you, maybe it was something you needed to share with me. Man please, forget you. You a typical li'l hood chick and I'm not down for it. I'm done with you." He gave a snide laugh, "You play too many games and you too confused. I don't have no time for that. I got enough problems and I don't need to pick up no new ones. So since you so busy lyin'," he waved his hand under his chin, "I'ma step. Shoulda known you were a liar."

"A liar?"

"Yeah, a liar. You ridiculous."

Tears filled my eyes. "You got a whole lotta nerve, like you so stand up and self-righteous. I'ma liar, you wait right here!"

"Ma, please. I'm out. I ain't waitin' for you no more, I've waited enough."

"Leave if you want to and see what happens!" I didn't know what I would or even could do, but I felt like if he took one step off this porch I was gon' hurt him. I stormed into the house, picked up my baby out of his crib and walked back to the porch. "He is why I've been canceling dates with you! It wasn't about no other dude, or about me lying!"

"You got a baby?"

"Yeah, I do. And that was his deadbeat-ass daddy in the store with me, not my man. I can't stand him. He doesn't take care of his son, he does nothing, which means this baby is all mine. Period. So yes, I'ma statistic and now that you know, what you can do," I flicked my hand as if I'd just performed a magic trick, "is step."

"Toi—"

"What you calling me for? Didn't you say you didn't deal with statistics?"

"Yeah, but—"

"Ain't no but, 'cause that's the ignorant shit you said. Now get off my porch and go home!"

We stood there for a moment, the very moment that I knew we would always meet. And the longer we stood there saying nothing, the more I felt like a fool. I looked at Harlem and shook my head. I turned to go inside and slammed the door behind me. A few seconds later, I heard him get in his Jeep and leave.

* * *

I sat down on the couch and instead of falling to pieces, I hunched my knees almost to my chest and placed my son in the space between and stared at him. "I love you, you know that?" I paused as if I were waiting for an answer and the most I got was a few grunts and groans. For a moment I thought he was going to the bathroom, so I started to laugh. "Nasty boy, Noah." I ran my hands over his head. "I will never deny you again. If a man can't accept you, then he can't accept me. I still don't know what we gon' do with each other. All I know is that we in this together." I started tickling him, he started laughing and eventually I started laughing, too. And for a moment, I forgot about my mother, welfare, Qua, Harlem, and all the other problems I had. All that mattered for right now was my son and seeing him smile.

An hour into playing with Noah, he fell asleep in my arms. I went in my room, lay him on my bed, and turned on the TV. A repeat of Keyshia Cole's reality show was playing.

Seven came into my room. "Yo, I'm leaving. Man-Man is across the street with Shae's little brothers."

"Ai'ight, lock the door behind you," I said.

After a while, I sat wondering if I should call Harlem. But then I figured, what for? Maybe my mother was right. Maybe I didn't have time for everything I wanted to do, or better yet, used to and just maybe boys were included.

A few minutes into my thoughts, the doorbell rang and it scared me. I sucked my teeth. If this was Man-Man I was gon' strangle him. I placed pillows around my son then hopped off the bed, stormed down the hall and snatched the door open.

Harlem was standing there. Out of fear of being thrown off balance because I was so shocked to see him again, I leaned against the back of the door.

"I tried," he hunched his shoulders, "to say forget you. But every time I drove closer to my dorm, something kept bringing me back down your block so—you know I guess I was meant to be here."

"So what you saying?" I hoped he couldn't hear my heart skipping a thousand beats.

"I don't know what I'm saying. All I know is that I can't stop thinking about you, wanting to be with you, wanting to spend time with you. And I miss you like crazy."

"You're not mad?"

His eyes widened, "Am I mad? Hell yeah! You lied to me." He pointed his hands like a gun in my face.

I held my head down quickly and looked back up at him.

He had a look of disgust on his face, but underneath I could tell that he still cared for me, otherwise why would he be here? Right? At least I pray I was right.

"Toi," he continued, "you had me thinking one thing and it was something completely different. I mean, really, I could look at you and say is Toi really your name?"

"What kind of question is that? You got a lot of nerve. It's not like you ever asked and then the day I was going to tell you, you came out with some statistics bullshit. Heck, how would you feel? You didn't exactly make falling in love with you and telling you the truth easy for me!" Without warning, tears streamed down my face. "Know what? It's obvious that this is going nowhere so why are you even here?"

He walked up close to me. "You in love with me?"

"It doesn't even matter."

He kissed my tears away. "Yes it does."

"Why?"

"Because I want to be here. And leaving you alone is not that easy."

"Well, I have a baby."

"I know."

"And I can't continue to be ashamed of that."

"I don't expect you to."

"So then, like I said before, what exactly are you saying?"

"I'm saying," he grabbed my hand and pulled me closer to him, "I'm here. And I don't know what this means or where this is going, but I care about you and right now leaving you alone is not something I want to do. So what you think? You believe in second chances?"

"Yeah," I smiled, "actually I do."

"Cool, so introduce me to your little boy so we can hurry and order some Chinese food. I'm starving."

Drama Part III

The Game Done Changed

14

"Harlem," I spoke slowly into the phone because my head ached like crazy. My mother was off this weekend and at the spur of the moment she decided she wanted to drive to North Carolina to visit some of our relatives, a trip that I couldn't make. After all, I had to work. Then I woke up this morning feeling horrible. My head was banging and my body ached. I thought maybe I was having a bad case of cramps but my period had just gone off last week, so that wasn't it. Needless to say, I was on the phone with Harlem, canceling yet another date and this one, we were supposed to do with Noah. "I'm sick as a dog."

"I hear you, what's wrong?"

"I don't know, I just hurt all over. Like I have the flu or something."

"Where's the baby?"

"He's here."

"How are you taking care of him if you're sick?"

"I'll be okay, but look," I felt myself about to throw up, "I gotta go." I don't remember if I hung up the phone or not. I ran to the bathroom and it seemed that everything I'd ever eaten splattered all on the floor. It was official, I was a mess.

After a few minutes of wondering exactly how I was going to do this, my bell rang and I dragged myself to answer it. I didn't ask who it was, I simply opened the door.

"You alright, ma?"

It was Harlem. I couldn't believe he was over here and I was looking like a stray dog. But the way I felt, I didn't even care. "Har—" and before I could finish I was throwing up, leaving a trail on the living room floor to the bathroom.

"Damn ma, you fucked up." I couldn't tell if he wanted to laugh or felt sorry for me.

"Whatever," I said wiping specks of vomit from the corners of my mouth as I came back to the living room.

"Ai'ight," he laid his baseball cap on the edge of the couch, "I'ma help you out."

"It's cool," I said, feeling a sudden burst of chills run through my body.

"Pretty Girl, look at you. You're shivering. Where's Noah?"

I pointed down the hall. "He's on the floor playing."

Harlem helped me to the bed and said, "Get in. Ya man got this."

I smiled at him. He was so cute but there was no way he could help. He was sure to simply be in my way.

"You called out sick?" he asked.

"No, I need the money. I have to try and go to work."

"Girl, please," Harlem looked at me and frowned. "Anything you need, I got you." He placed a hundred dollar bill on my nightstand. "You staying home today." He looked at Noah. "Right?"

Noah smiled and Harlem said, "My man." He smiled back at the baby, then looked back at me. "You take anything?"

"No."

"You need some Tylenol and maybe some soup. I'ma walk to the corner store and get you some. Where are his clothes?"

"In the closet. Why?"

"Because we're going to the store to get you some medicine and soup."

"Oh no," I said, clearing my throat, "he's a real funny baby and he's particular about who he goes out with. He'll start crying." By the time I finished giving my spiel Harlem had Noah dressed and was waving bye-bye. "Be careful, Harlem."

"I got you ma."

I'll admit I was a little concerned about Harlem being with my baby. Not because I thought he would do something to him. But because I didn't feel like he's ever taken care of a baby and I didn't want him experimenting with mine. After a few minutes, they returned with Tylenol, a can of chicken noodle soup, and juice.

Harlem warmed the soup and gave me the Tylenol and the juice. Afterwards he sat on the floor and played with Noah. I couldn't believe that I'd been this lucky. This was more than I could ever have dreamed, even if I was too sick to enjoy it.

Harlem started to sniff. "Toi" He sniffed again. "You smell that?"

Yeah, I smelled it, but heck, I was sick. I quickly shut my eyes and then when he wasn't looking, I peeled one of them open. Harlem looked at Noah. "Oh no." He bent down and sniffed Noah. "My man, you stink. Aw man, you playin' me out, son."

Noah smiled.

"Damn, man." Harlem said, getting Noah's Pampers, wipes, and powder.

"Now how I'm 'spose to do this?" he looked at the Pamper as if he were studying Greek. "Ai'ight, this must be the front." He lay Noah on the floor and went to take his Pamper off, then Harlem looked at the mess in Noah's Pamper. "Wait a minute. I better not do that." So he left the Pamper open. "Okay, how I'ma do this?" As he looked at Noah, Noah began to pee. "Yo son!" he jumped up. "Yo Toi, wake up! My man just pissed in my face."

126

I was laughing so hard that I practically fell out the bed. I got out of the bed and took the Pamper from him. "Give me my child."

"Yo Toi, he don't know me like that." Harlem looked down at his shirt. I gave him a baby wipe to clean up. "Look at my shirt."

"Just take it off," I said.

"You being fresh."

"Boy, please. You think I've never seen a man before?"

"You ain't never seen me before."

"Whatever," I said as he eased his shirt over his head. All I could say was have mercy. Mountains and mountains of muscles were everywhere. Harlem caught me looking his body over and he locked into my gaze. We stared at each other for a moment and then he said, "Get back in the bed. I got it from here."

He and Noah played on the floor as I drifted off. When I awoke, toys were everywhere, the TV was playing and Harlem and Noah lay in the middle of the floor knocked out with Noah asleep on Harlem's chest. Amazingly, I was feeling a lot better. "Harlem," I whispered, while looking at the clock and seeing that it was midnight, "wake up."

Harlem's eyes peeled open and he wiped the corner of his mouth. "Yo, I fell asleep. Pretty Girl, I gotta give you credit; homeboy is a lot of work."

"Really?"

"He was cool, though," Harlem said, laying next to me in the bed and placing Noah between us.

"But this is my man." He kissed me on my forehead. "I think I could probably do this."

128   For the first time in my life I felt like Heaven was smiling. I thought about telling Harlem that I loved him, but then a part of me still wasn't sure where this was going, so I changed my mind . . . though there was nothing I could do about my heart.

15

"So," my mother said as we sat at the kitchen table planning the guest list for Cousin Shake's birthday dinner. "Have you two thought about what college you're going to apply to?"

"I want to go to Spelman," Seven said, as if her mind was already made up. "And with my grades and honors status, I should be able to apply for a scholarship."

"And you?" my mother turned to me.

"Maybe I'll do some hair or something. I don't know."

"Is that what you want to do?" my mother asked. "I thought you wanted to be a teacher?"

"I do."

"Well, you have to go to a four-year college for that."

"Ma," I tilted my head to the side, "how I'ma go

to college and I can barely get a babysitter to go to the corner store?"

"You're exaggerating."

"I'm so serious."

"Some colleges have daycares right on campus, Toi, and Spelman is one of them."

"Ma, we live in Jersey."

"Well . . . I was thinking . . . Cousin Shake, your daddy, and I were all talking, and I was seriously considering putting in transfer papers to the Atlanta office. Your father even said he would come and help us move."

"Yeah, I'm sure," Seven said snidely. "That's his specialty, moving."

"You know he's not with his girlfriend anymore."

"Sounds personal," Seven snapped. I could tell by her tone that she was still hurt by our parents splitting up, especially since my father left my mother for another woman and had a baby with her.

"Seven," my mother looked at her, "you need to stop that. Your father loves you. Yes, he was wrong, but he's really trying and you need to give him a chance."

"After what he did to you?"

"Even after what he did to me. So, maybe you girls ought to apply to Spelman, as well as some other colleges. I know that's where you want to go, but never put all your eggs in one basket."

I twisted my lips. "Okay."

"You know I'll apply. Matter of fact, my application is already filled out." Seven smiled.

"Alright," my mother tapped her pen against Cousin Shake's guest list. "We need to invite Cousin Shake's new girlfriend, Ms. Minnie."

"Ms. Minnie! Ma, do we have to?"

"Toi!" my mother snapped.

"Oh . . . my . . . God!"

16

It was awkward at first, dating and having a baby, but then eventually we worked the kinks out. Like, how do you ask your boyfriend to hold your baby so you can go to the bathroom? Well, I discovered you just ask him. And how do you tell your boyfriend that you have to place the car seat in his back seat when his car is his prize possession and you know the bottom of the car seat will leave a mark? Well, you have to do what you have to do.

And since I liked Harlem, I wanted to see how we could work this out. My mother was sort of wishy washy. Yeah, she thought Harlem was a cool dude, and she respected the way he took us all out, but some things she wasn't really crazy about. For some reason I felt like if he broke my heart, it would hurt her more than it would me.

"Harlem," I said as we sat at Applebee's, "have you ever broken a girl's heart?"

He looked at me funny. "Why?"

"Because . . . I'm just wondering like, where is all this going to go?"

"Just flow with it Toi."

"How?"

"Harlem, wassup," a male voice cut me short. I looked over and there were three cats giving Harlem a pound.

"What's good, ma?" One of them spoke to me, while the others nodded their heads.

I smiled.

"This is Toi," Harlem said.

"Yo, this you, Harlem?" another asked, while pointing to me and then to Noah. "You somebody's daddy?"

"Man, please. Look at me. You know I ain't nobody's daddy. You know me better than that."

What did he just say? I looked at my son, who was now sucking on the end of his toy. He smiled at me. I wanted to punch Harlem straight in his gut, and if I could stop my hands from shaking, I would do it. Instantly, I had an attitude. In the midst of Harlem talking to his friends, the waitress brought our food.

"Ai'ight, man," one of them said. "Check you tomorrow."

"Cool."

As they walked away, Harlem said, "Those my dudes from school."

"That's nice," I snapped, while raking my fork across my salad.

"You alright?"

"It doesn't even matter." I rolled my eyes as my cell phone rang. "Hello?" I answered.

"Toi, this is Quamir."

"Yeah."

"Yo, I wanna see you."

"Lose yourself." And I hung up.

Harlem tilted his head. "Who was that? A dude?" For a moment I thought he was jealous.

I sighed. "Yeah, it was."

"Oh, so you talking to other cats?"

"It was his daddy or did you forget he had one?"

Harlem sat silent for a moment. "Yo, listen, my fault. I didn't mean a thing by what I said a minute ago."

"Yes, you did. So don't apologize for something you meant to say."

"But Toi," Harlem said, "give me credit for something. You know I'm trying and you know this is all new to me."

"Don't worry, Harlem, because I see it's about to get old real quick."

"Toi—"

"Look, I'm just ready to go home."

We ate the rest of our meal in silence and then got in the car and left. I could tell that Harlem felt some type of way, and so did I. But I'd denied my son long enough, and I wasn't going to do it again.

We stopped in front of my house and he helped

me out of the car. Usually, I would've kissed him goodnight, but tonight I didn't. Instead, I went in to the house, where my mother was sitting reading a book. "Where's Harlem?"

He waved from the door. "Hi, Mrs. McKnight."

"How you doing baby? Listen, I would like to invite you and your family over here for Cousin Shake's surprise birthday party. Toi's dad will be here and I think it'll be a lot of fun."

"Cool, I'll bring my mother."

"Great, I'd love to meet her."

"Okay, we'll be here." He smiled. "Ai'ight, Toi. I'm leaving."

"Yeah, you do that." And I proceeded to undress Noah.

"That was rude," my mother said after Harlem left.

"You don't even know what he said . . . telling me that—"

"Wait a minute. Who are you talking to?"

Instantly, I brought it down. "My fault."

"It was gon' have to be somebody's fault, 'cause in a minute I would be explaining to the judge why all your teeth were missing."

She always had to go overboard.

"So what's the problem?" she asked.

"Let me tell you what Harlem said to me . . ." and I told her what happened at the restaurant.

"Well, I'm a little surprised because I really like Harlem, but what you have to understand is that not every guy is meant to be around your child.

I'm sure he didn't mean any harm and he apologized, right?"

"Yes."

"Well then, give him another chance and if it happens again, then you may want to rethink the relationship."

"Yeah ma," I said with a drag, "I guess you're right."

"Of course I am. That's why I leave my boo outside."

I smiled. "What boo? Ma, you got a boo?"

"What? You ain't know?" She rose from her seat. "Y'all better stop sleeping on your mama."

"Ma!" I yelled behind her.

"Hollah!"

17

"Surprise!" Everyone yelled as Cousin Shake walked into the house, looking like he was really surprised. We all knew he'd been sneaking around and bribed Man-Man for the date of the party. Instantly, Cousin Shake started doing a bunch of jailhouse poses for the camera.

"Good thing I'm always sharp," he said, spinning around, breaking into another pose. "Or y'all mighta caught me off guard."

I shook my head—just when I thought his clothes couldn't get any worse, he took it there. He wore a two-piece Hawaiian short set with palm trees that lit up and flashed like a cheap motel sign. "I can't believe that y'all did all this for me. I feel, I feel, good." And he proceeded to do the DC slide while rapping, "A hip-hop-a hipida-hipida-hip hop you don't stop . . . a rockin'."

Oh . . . kaaaay.

"Do it Roscoe Shaka-deen Green!" Ms. Minnie screamed while holding her arms out and shaking like she was having a seizure. "You so sharp, you 'bout to stab me, leave me on the ground bleeding, and the next thing I know all my arteries gon' be carved out, and I'm laying there shaking. *Baby,* you so sharp I know yo whole outfit is 'bout to straight crip on a fool!"

"Mama," Percy tried to whisper, "you embarrassing me in front of my in-laws."

In-laws? Oh hell no.

"Ma," I said, tight-lipped, "told you we shouldn't have invited them."

"Be quiet. Cousin Shake said he really likes Ms. Minnie."

"Ma, he can't see Ms. Minnie."

"Shut up." She laughed. "She's not that short. Now be nice."

Just then the doorbell rang. "I'll get it." I walked to the door feeling nervous and anxious at the same time. I knew it was Harlem and this was the first time he would be having dinner with my family. When I opened the door, there stood Harlem and his mother.

"Hi."

"Toi?" she said. "I've heard so much about you."

Don't ask me why, but I hugged her. After our embrace, I turned toward my family and introduced her to everyone. "This is Ms. Simms. She's moving to Atlanta, too."

"Oh wow." My mother shook her hand. "Nice to meet you. We may be moving to Atlanta as well."

"Really?" Ms. Simms responded. "Well, we'll have to chat. Atlanta is wonderful!"

As my mother and Ms. Simms began talking, the doorbell rang again. I opened it and there was my daddy, smiling with two suitcases in his hands. "All that's for Cousin Shake?" I asked.

"Your mother didn't tell you?" he said.

"Tell me what?"

"I'm home again."

"Home? I thought she had a boo."

My mother walked over to the door and gave me half a grin. "Mind your business. Come in, Tre." I just looked at them. And they call *me* crazy.

I could tell that Seven had an attitude, but she tried to keep a smile on her face as she chatted with Josiah and his mother.

"Toi, I need to tell you something," Harlem said as everyone entered the dining room so we could eat dinner.

"What is it?" I said.

"My mother doesn't know—"

"Dinner is set," my mother said, cutting us off. "Toi, I need you to grab the hot cider."

"I'll be back," I said to Harlem, holding my index finger up.

"But Toi—"

"One minute."

"You have a beautiful home, Grier." I could over hear Ms. Simms complimenting my mother.

"Thank you. I've been looking at some houses on the internet in Atlanta. I'm hoping to find something similar."

"You will love Atlanta. I need some girls to chat it up with." She paused. "This food smells delicious."

"Thank you," my mother said. "And Minnie made the Sock It To Me cake."

"'Cause she knows," Cousin Shake said as if he were making an announcement, "that sockin' it to me is my favorite. Bam . . . bam . . . bam . . ." he said, running in place.

I'ma be sick.

"I want a big ole slice of that," Man-Man insisted.

"I put my foot all up in that." Ms. Minnie smiled, showing the gold caps in front of her mouth.

"Mama." Percy groaned.

"Shut up, Lil' Bootsy and sit up straight in that booster seat before you fall over the side." She looked at my mother, Josiah's mother, and Ms. Simms. "I don't know about y'all, but chil'ren works me. That's why I got one," she held her index finger up, "and he gon' mess around and I'ma flip his behind down the stairs, out the door, take him across the street, put him on the bus, and tell him don't come back."

"Mama, why you got to say all that? Why you can't tell a simple story?"

"Better break yo'self, fool."

"Seven," my father leaned over and said under

his breath, "is that your boyfriend?" He pointed to Percy. "And his mama?"

"Daddy, you got a better chance of him being with Man-Man."

"Alright now, Seven," my father said sternly.

Seven pointed to Josiah and his mother. "That's my boo and his crew."

Cousin Shake cleared his throat and stood up. "Fo' anybody eat, fo' anybody eat, I feel a need for Jesus up in this piece. Er'body stand up."

"Regulate baby," Ms. Minnie wiggled her neck. "Reg . . . u . . . late."

"What is she talking about?" I whispered to my mother.

"I don't know."

That's when I realized that Cousin Shake was about to pray. Immediately, I looked at my mother. I couldn't help it; it just slipped out. "Ma, you promised."

"Can we sit down for this?" Seven rolled her eyes to the ceiling.

"We got a problem here?" Cousin Shake snapped. Nobody responded, so he continued. "Now er'-body hold hands and bow they heads," Cousin Shake said, and reluctantly we all did as he asked. "Hmmmmmm," Cousin Shake started to moan. "We are gathered here today . . . hmmmm . . . in the sight of this holy matrimony of turkey, rice, and gravy—"

"Hallelujah!" Ms. Minnie added.

"Hmmmmmm," Cousin Shake continued. "We thank you Jesus Crisco."

"It's Christ," Seven interrupted. Cousin Shake looked at her as if he could slap her. "I'm just saying, it's Christ."

"Continue, Cousin Shake," my mother said.

"Hmmmmm and we wanna thank you for blessing me on my twenty-ninth birthday."

"Twenty-ninth?" everybody said simultaneously.

"That's what he said, ain't it?" Ms. Minnie snapped as if she dared us to say something different. "Go on Roscoe Shaka-deen."

"And we wanna thank you," Cousin Shake continued on, "for the disciplines, Mark, Matthew, Luke, and Bobby."

"Who is Bobby?" Man-Man looked around and asked.

Cousin Shake ignored him. "Hmmmmm and we wanna ask you to watch over the homeless, the poor, the ones who got more money than I do, the fool who stole my knock-off Rolex. It might not've meant nothing to them, but it meant something to me. Watch over the li'l chil'ren, and all the crackheads, and get at the man in the meat market for selling that rotten beef. And see about Paco over there in the bodega and tell him he needs to learn how to speak English. Stop by and see about the all the stray dogs and the cats. Turn this mother out and show all the children that Margaret was a virgin."

"Who is Margaret?" Man-Man looked at my daddy.

"See about my baby mama," Cousin Shake continued on. "Let her know our baby is forty-nine years old and it's time for her to let the child support go. Come on down Jonathan—I mean Jesus. We need you. Amen."

"I think it's Christmas," Seven mumbled as we sat down to eat.

"Be quiet," my mother gave her the evil eye. "Toi," my mother looked at me. "I think I hear Noah crying."

"Excuse me." I went to my room, picked Noah up and brought him back into the dining room.

"He's old enough now, Toi," my mother said. "He can eat a little mashed potatoes."

"Oh wow," Ms. Simms said, "how adorable. So Grier, you have two girls and two boys."

"No, I have two girls and one boy." My mother slapped Man-Man on the back of his head for eating with his fingers. "The baby is my grandson."

"Oh wow," Ms. Simms looked at Seven. "You have a beautiful baby."

We all laughed.

"Ms. Simms," I said, "Noah is my son." Immediately, her face changed to a disgusted shock. She looked at Harlem. "You never told me Toi had a baby."

"What's the problem?" Cousin Shake asked. "They a package deal."

"Yeah," Ms. Minnie said. "We got a problem here?"

"Oh no." Ms. Simms cleared her throat. "It's no problem. And they should be a package deal. I completely understand."

I felt so embarrassed. It was obvious that Ms. Simms wasn't pleased with me having a baby. I couldn't believe that Harlem didn't say anything to her. We all ate dinner, and although we laughed and joked, my feelings were really hurt. Once dessert was served and everyone started holding their own conversations, I whispered to Harlem, "Why didn't you tell your mother?"

"I didn't get around to it. That's it, Toi. No other reason."

"Well, she didn't seem too pleased with it."

"Don't worry about my mother. Worry about me." He took Noah out of my hands, "'cause I ain't going nowhere."

For the rest of the party we had a good time, but I could tell that Ms. Simms was still upset.

18

"You're not staying here, Tre." I woke up to my parents' arguing. It was almost like old times again. "No way."

"Listen," my father tried to speak quietly. "I wanna work things out with you."

"Man, if you don't get out my face," she spat. I could hear her shuffling around in the kitchen. "I'm raising two women in here and they know what you put me through. If I let you just walk back into my life when you've showed me nothing that says you've changed or even deserve another chance, then what does that say to do them? That any man who begs should come back? No, not. I have a life and I will not have you interrupting it."

"But I told you I was moving to Atlanta. I wanted to be closer to you when you move there."

"I didn't confirm Atlanta with you. Look, you're here. Enjoy your children and that's it. But after last night I don't want you in my bed. Now excuse me—I have to get ready for work."

"Ahhhhhhh!!!!!!" Cousin Shake screamed. I jumped out the bed and ran into the kitchen. When I got in there, I saw that everybody except my brother, who was on the porch selling Kool-Aid to a line of kids that wrapped around my mother's porch, was in a panic. Cousin Shake was standing in the kitchen with a zebra print body suit on. "Somebody done been in my stash of Passion Fruit Alizé."

"What?" my mother blinked, half-shielding her eyes while looking at Cousin Shake.

"You heard me, It's gone. I was feeding my tender some grapes and went to pour some Alizé all over her fifty-year-old body and I was hit. De . . . ple . . . ted."

"What in the world?" my mother said. Just then the doorbell rang.

"I'll get it," Seven said. "Ma!" she yelled, "it's for you."

"Who is it?"

"It's Ms. Margarite from down the street."

My mother stormed to the door. She couldn't stand Ms. Margarite. "I just want you to know," Ms. Margarite said, "that all these kids outside on your porch is drunk! So much for your little Prince and his Kool-Aid stand."

"What?" my mother snapped. "Amir!" she screamed, "get in here!"

Man-Man came inside, smiling a little too hard and a little too animated. It was a dead giveaway. We'd found exactly who'd ripped Cousin Shake off. "My apologies, Margarite," my mother said. "I will take care of this."

And the next thing I knew, all I could see was dust flying as my mother dug into Man-Man's behind. When she was done, she blew the residue from her cuticles and he lay stretched out on the floor, looking as if all he needed was a white sheet draped over him.

19

Ever since Cousin Shake's party, Harlem had been acting funny. He claimed that he wasn't, but I could see the difference. We argued about everything and every time I said I'm going to leave him alone, I never do.

"You ready to go to the mall?" Harlem asked as he walked into my room. "Unless you want your new boyfriend to take you."

"Don't play," I spat at Harlem while picking up Noah. "Are you ready?"

"See how she cuttin' me off," Harlem said to Noah. "Tell me, is your mommy on the creep?" He looked in Noah's eyes. "You'd tell your daddy—" I knew he'd caught himself as soon as he said it.

The word daddy stuck in my ears and rang like a bad tune. I'd never thought of my son calling anybody daddy, especially since the meaning of the word turned out to equate to being hurt, at least to me, a hurt I didn't want my son having to deal with. "You mean *Harlem,* not daddy."

Harlem stood there for a moment, and just from the look on his face, I knew I'd hurt his feelings. But this was my son we were talking about, and suppose Harlem and I broke up one day. Then what? Noah would walk around here calling every man daddy? Please. So to avoid all that, we wouldn't even start it.

"Yeah, you right," Harlem remarked. "I meant Harlem."

We stood there in a moment of awkward silence, staring at each other. "You still going to the mall or not?" he snapped, handing the baby to me. "Otherwise, I'ma bounce."

"Yeah . . . I want to go to the mall, but if you don't—"

"Well, let's go then. I got something to do." I went to hand Noah back to him and instead of taking him he said, "I'll meet you in the car, Toi."

For at least fifteen minutes we drove in dead silence. No radio playing, no CD. All we heard was the crackling of his leather seats as I crossed one leg over the other and back again. I looked at Harlem and twisted my mouth. Before I could ask him what was his problem, Noah started crying, so I turned toward the back seat. I couldn't find his pacifier anywhere back there but I knew there was one in the middle console. "Could you hand me his pacifier?" I asked.

IF I WAS YOUR GIRL

And when I turned around to retrieve it, Harlem tossed it at me, just missing hitting my face. I snatched it mid-air and gave him the evil eye before placing the pacifier in Noah's mouth. Instantly, he was quiet. I turned back to Harlem. "What is yo problem?"

"Go 'head, Toi," he snapped, getting off the exit.

"Go 'head what?"

"This is exactly why," he shook his head, "I didn't want to get involved."

"So what, you wanna bounce?"

"Maybe," he said as his phone rang, and instead of letting it go to voicemail or placing it on vibrate, like he usually did, he answered it. Don't ask me why but my heart pounded. I thought I heard a female voice, but I wasn't sure. Maybe I was straining too hard, and since I really couldn't hear the other end well, I watched Harlem's face and listened closely to what he had to say, for confirmation. As soon as he started to smile and his words oozed out his mouth, I knew he was talking to another girl.

I felt stupid—scratch that, stupid didn't even fit right then, after thinking he was perfect. I couldn't believe that I was sitting there watching him kick it to a chick.

"Yo," he said into the phone with ease. "I just been busy that's all . . . don't be like that . . . you know that's not even the case . . ." I was sick to my stomach and yes, he was sitting there with me and not her . . . but my chest still felt cold in the center. All the times that Quamir kicked it with a chick in my face tortured my mind and I was boiling over. I couldn't do it anymore. "Are you gon' kick it wit' your girl all night—or we gon' deal with this?" And I said it loud enough so whoever he was talking to could hear me clearly.

Harlem looked at me like I was crazy and I'm sure he could see the tears welling behind my eyes. "This is my friend," he said, "she's like a sister to me."

"A friend?" I cocked my neck to the side. "I been kickin' it with you for a minute now and all of a sudden you got a friend?"

"Yes, a friend." He pulled into the parking lot and placed the car in Park.

He returned his attention to the phone. "It's cool," he continued his conversation. I promise you, I wanted to scream. I hated female friends with a passion. They played your boyfriend against you. They knew all his male friends, they were always so accessible, and they thought they could tell your boyfriend about you. As far as I was concerned, they were nothin' but rejected broads he didn't or wouldn't kick it to.

"Well then, tell your friend to come and be your girl, 'cause I'm done." I reached for my purse and Noah's baby bag. I wasn't doing this again.

"Yo, let me talk to you later." And Harlem hung up the phone. "Where are you going?" he asked me.

"Home."

"Home?" he smirked. "Man, I'm not playing with you."

"Tell it to your li'l friend."

"Toi, it was nothin'."

"Yeah, that's what my daddy told my mother right before he moved to California and started a whole new family."

"That hurt you, huh?"

"What you think?" I snapped. My sight was blurry with tears. They felt like the New Orleans levees.

Plain and simple, I felt like shit. I knew he was talking to another chick and I wasn't about to sit there and take it. Honestly, it was almost like a part of me expected it. Harlem looked at me. I didn't know what hurt more, what he did or the memory of what Quamir had done. I turned toward the window, while doing my best to restrain the tears bubbling in my eyes. He gently grasped my chin and turned my face toward him. "Yo, listen. I didn't mean to hurt you."

"But you did and you disrespected me. And I'm not beat to be treated like less than what I am, so if you have plans on doing what you did again, then what I'ma do is take my baby and we gon' jet. Then you can go get your so-called friend and y'all can chill. Besides, didn't you just say you wanted to bounce?"

"I didn't mean that."

I could tell he was sincere, but I didn't care.

"What, you don't love me no more?" he said.

"I'm not even gon' acknowledge that." If he wasn't so big, I would slap him.

"Why you denying how you feel?"

"I'm not denying how I feel. You wanna know how I feel? I feel stupid and dumb, like this is a set-up for me to be played again. Well, guess what? Not this time. Oh, trust me, I'm so good on you. Besides, this doesn't mean nothin' to you. You ain't sleeping with me."

"Sleeping with you? What are you talking about?"

"Whatever."

"Yo, if you got something you wanna know or you wanna ask, then you ask me. Don't be slingin' no b.s. at me!"

"Why haven't we ever had sex, Harlem?"

"What, you feeling insecure? So tell me, Toi, when you suggest we have it? Before or after your mother walks in, or better yet, when Cousin Shake gives his speech of you ain't got to go home but you gotta get the hell outta here. Yo, I'm good. When I want some, I'll let you know. So chill."

"Chill? You are such a liar. You know there's times when they're not home and it's just you and me. You know my mother works at night."

"Yo, what is this?" His jaw twitched. He was really pissed.

"I don't know. You tell me."

"Know what, Toi, I don't even see you right now." Harlem hopped out his truck and took Noah out the back seat. "Another thing, you got a budget today."

"Oh, you mad so I have a budget?"

"Yeah, 'cause you too wild with spending money. You got a son and you need to save. Suppose I ain't here one day?"

"You plan on leaving?"

"You plan on pushing me away?"

Before I could respond, I heard, "You so silly," float from behind me. "I'm so glad we're having a girl." Instinctively, I turned around. Quamir and some pregnant girl I'd never seen were behind me.

Quamir stared at me long and hard, then he diverted his gaze from me to Harlem then back again. And if I'm not mistaken, he had an attitude because Harlem was holding Noah. This had to be a joke.

"There go his father," Harlem said snidely. "Excuse me, his daddy."

"I see him."

Nobody said anything to the other. We let our silence speak for us as we walked into the mall. Truthfully, I didn't even feel like looking in any of the stores. But I just did it anyway to pass the time. I may have been mad, but I still wanted Harlem around.

We passed a few more stores, ate at the food court practically in silence and then I couldn't take it anymore, so I said, "I'm ready to go."

"Cool," he said and we left.

Once we got to my house, Tay was there sitting on the porch. She asked if she could take Noah to her little cousin's birthday party. After giving her some extra bottles and Pampers, Harlem and I were left alone. No one was home, except us, and we went to my room. "I'm so sick of making the same mistakes over and over again," I said more to myself than to Harlem, but I'd said it loud enough for him to hear.

Harlem looked at me like I was crazy. "What are you talking about?"

"I'm just tired of bullshit."

"Bullshit? Whose bullshit? Yo, say what you been dyin' to say all day."

"I'm sayin' it!" I snapped.

"You ain't sayin' shit."

"What you care for? Everyone knows you're ashamed of me."

"What the . . ." He looked at me crazy. "Yo, I gotta go."

"What you runnin' for?"

"I'm not runnin' but you got issues. You don't need a man right now. You need to deal with you."

"So why haven't you answered my questions? Since I'm so wrong—"

"Because I can't believe you."

"I knew you were gon' leave anyway, so whatever." My throat was trembling. "Harlem . . . whatever."

"Is that your answer to everything? Whatever? Let me tell you something I fell for you, because I thought you were about something. I was diggin' you before I knew you had a son. But once I saw you with him, you reminded me of my mom, so I felt at home with you. You ain't the only chick in the world, Toi, but you the only one I want. I can't believe that I been around your family, went against my own bond, fell for you, and here you are acting like this. Yo for real. I'm out."

I felt anxious; I knew if he left I would never see him again. And maybe this actually meant I needed to let him leave so that I could collect me, but I couldn't. My head was spent. Was it a crime if I didn't want to be alone? I truly needed some space and time where I could grow and just belong to me. I'd belonged to Noah, to my mother, to the welfare office, even a part of me still belonged to Quamir, but Harlem was for me. And at this moment, if at no other moment, I felt like he wanted me for me. "Don't leave Harlem, please. I'm so so sorry. Please don't go."

"Nah, ma. I need to breathe. I just caught myself. I was slippin'."

I rushed to the door and blocked his pathway. "Harlem, please. Don't leave."

Harlem took a deep breath and sat on the edge of my bed. He didn't open his mouth. I could tell that I'd cut him deep, but what more could I say? The men in my life always turned out to have some type of game with them. My father was a cheater, Quamir was a cheater, a drug dealer, you name it. Now I had Harlem, who I could put money on would break my heart. I sniffed and stepped to the side. "Harlem, it's cool, you can go. My fault. I'm not gon' hold you back."

He let out a long breath of air, rose from the bed and walked toward the door, where he stopped in front of me. "I don't know what I'm doing with you. I'm not even supposed to be here. I was supposed to kick it to you, chill wit' you for a minute and bounce. Yo, this is crazy."

Tears were pouring down my face as Harlem pulled me close and began kissing them off. "You know you're my boo," he said, kissing me on the mouth. His kisses were so warm and his touch so comforting that I didn't want him to stop. I ran my hands up Harlem's back and lifted his shirt up. "Ma," he sighed. "I don't know."

I locked my door. "I know." I kissed him on his chest and as I began to undress him, he was still reluctant, yet he started to undress me.

"What you doin', ma? Your mother gon' come down here."

"She's at work." I led him by the hand and he followed me to the bed. And when we were done, he held me tight and simply looked at me.

After an hour of lying in his arms, he said, "I wanna tell you something—"

"I feel really bad about the way I acted." I cut him off.

"Just listen," he placed his index finger to my lips. "I'm going back to Atlanta."

"What?" *Did he just say he was moving back to Atlanta?*

"Yeah . . . and I was hoping that you would meet me there."

"Pssst, please." I sucked my teeth. "What is this supposed to be, Shakespeare? Boy, please, this is the hood. Romeo and Juliet got killed last year."

"I'm serious."

"Me too."

"Come on, Toi."

"Harlem, I have a whole school year before I even go to college."

"So I'll wait."

"You gon' wait for me?"

"Yes."

"Yeah, and what's your mother going to say about that?"

"It's my life. She just has to get used to the idea. I mean, it's a lot."

"What's a lot?"

"You having a baby."

"Really?"

"Yeah. She's not really feeling me having a ready-made family. But it's my decision."

"Whatever." I looked around the room at our clothes strewn on the floor. Maybe this was a mistake.

"Look," I said, getting out of bed and slipping my housecoat on. "You 'bout to bounce?"

He looked at me like I was crazy. "I guess so."

"Cool." I stood in silence, watching him get dressed. He went to kiss me on his way out and I turned my face. After he left, I showered and I cried myself to sleep.

20

"Are you sure Harlem is ready for all of this?" my mother asked as we sat to the dining room table.

"For all of what?" I said.

"For all you bring."

"Dang ma, you say that like I'ma problem."

"You're not a problem, Toi, but you are a package."

"Ma—"

"He didn't even tell his mother you had a baby," she looked at me, "and you've been dating for how long?"

"So what. You don't like him now?"

"No, that's not it. I like him, he's a nice guy. But I think he has some growing up to do, and so do you, before you two can handle a relationship and a baby."

"Ma, so, what you're saying is I should be lonely for the rest of my life?"

"Why are you putting words in my mouth?" She frowned. "I'm your mother, if I can't tell you about your mistakes, then who can? Harlem is a nice guy, but I don't like that he didn't tell his mother. I don't think he's ready for all of this."

"But ma, Harlem is always here. We go out . . . and with the baby . . . and why would he invite me over there for his mother's going away party if he wasn't ready?"

"Because he likes you, Toi. I just think he doesn't know what to do with you. You are a package, honey, and unfortunately sometimes boys at this age don't understand what it means to be with a teen mother with a baby. So—"

"Ma—"

She held her finger up for me to be quiet. "So, I just want you to take some time out for yourself, figure out not just what you want to do in life, but do it. There are going to be a million Harlems who all promise the same thing. 'If you were my girl'" she put on a animated male voice, "'I'd give you this and I'd give you that.' But at the end of the day, they may just walk away and if you haven't gotten things right for you and your son, you will have more crying times than you bargained for. Now, I love you—you know that. But I'm also a mother and I know that Harlem's mother didn't like you having a child. I also know that Harlem had to be embarrassed, and I also know that you haven't done what you need to do for you."

My mother was right. The problem was she was always right.

I sat there looking at her, trying my best not to think about what she'd just said. "You gon' still keep Noah for me?"

"Yes, I don't want my grandbaby over there around that lady. I didn't like her face when she found out he was your son," she said as the doorbell rang. "She might mess around and I'd have to beat her down."

"Okay, ma." I laughed. "You can fall back."

"Heyyyy!" Tay said as she walked into the kitchen. "Toi, Harlem is outside and he brought a friend. Hollah!"

"Hello." I went to kiss Ms. Simms on the cheek and she turned her face away. I looked at Tay and she said, "I will fight an old lady."

Harlem grabbed my hand. "Come in, come in." and led us into the family room. "This is my family," He pointed around. "My sister, my cousins and this is Toi," he said, "my girlfriend."

"Hello!" Harlem's sister smiled. "I've heard so much about you!"

"Really?" I blushed.

"Uhm hmm, too much," Ms. Simms said as she left the room.

I knew everyone in the room heard her because they became quiet. Then tried to resume their conversation, "So how've you've been, Toi?" Harlem's sister asked.

"Dinner is served," Ms. Simms said before I could answer.

As we walked into the dining room, Tay said, "This chick is trippin'. I don't wanna be here long."

"Chill, Tay. It's cool."

"No, it's not."

As we sat down at the table, Harlem said under his breath. "Toi, my mother's buggin'. Don't even pay that any mind."

"She doesn't like me having a baby."

"She doesn't have to be with you, I do."

If only that made me feel better. I ate very little and I knew Harlem noticed it.

"So what do you plan on doing with your life, Toi?" I looked up and Harlem's mother was staring at me.

"Where did that come from?" I asked.

"I'm just wondering what you're going to do after high school."

"I'm not sure . . ." I said, "if I'm going to college or not."

"Oh . . . kay. Is it just that you don't wanna go or what?"

"Well, before I had my son I got into a little bit of trouble, but I've been thinking about going to community college."

"Did you say trouble? Trouble for what?"

"Ai'ight, ma. That's enough," Harlem said.

"No, I'm just asking."

"Well, ask something else," he snapped.

"Who you talking to?" She arched her eyebrows.

"I'm talking to you."

"Excuse me?" Ms. Simms sputtered in disbelief. "Harlem," she slid from her chair from the table, "I need to see you in the kitchen."

"We gon' bounce after this." He gave me a slight massage on my shoulder as he walked out behind his mother.

As soon as they left the room, Tay leaned over to me and said, "We might need to roll up on moms."

"Calm down, Tay."

"I'm just sayin'. People looking like they wanna get it poppin'."

"Tay!"

"I'm just sayin'."

"Who are you talking to?" Ms. Simms screamed so loud it floated into the dining room.

"Ma, you being rude and I don't appreciate it. Toi's my girlfriend and this is how you treat her?"

"I told you not to bring her here and you did anyway. All she gon' do is have a buncha babies and be some—some—some two-dollar waitress somewhere for the rest of her life. Then she'll have you and all my hard earned money wrapped up in court in a buncha baby mama drama. Have me raising a buncha grandkids, 'cause she can't get off welfare!"

"How you know she's on welfare?"

"I can look at her and tell."

"You don't even know her! You foul, real foul!"

"And you're irresponsible! That girl is too fast for you. You don't even clean up your room and now you gon' play step-daddy. I'll be damned."

"I'm nineteen years old."

"And that's all you are. Let her eat dinner and take her home." I could hear her storming this way. "And the next time you raise your voice up in here—"

"Ma, please. You just bitter!"

When Harlem walked back into the dining room, he stopped suddenly because everybody was either looking at me or looking aimlessly around the room. I twisted my lips and placed my napkin on the table. "It's cool, Harlem. You can stay, I'll leave. Come on, Tay."

Ms. Simms stood there with a look of surprise on her face, like she didn't know that everyone heard her. "Uhmm, Toi, . . . I didn't mean to embarrass you. I just wanted—"

I cut her off. "Really, you don't have to explain anything to me. You were only protecting your son the same way I would protect mine. For real, no disrespect, but you need to check yourself, 'cause you really don't know me or my situation. I used to be ashamed of being a teen mom, but what I learned is that I'm in charge of me and what I do. So I no longer allow people like you to make me feel bad for who I am. 'Cause one thing for sure, I'ma damn good mother—I work, I go to school, and I take care of my son. Bon voyage!"

Tay stood up and snapped her fingers in a "z" motion. "Told yo ass. Come on, Harlem, and take us home." She tapped Harlem on his arm. "Move ya ass now. Don't start nothin', won't be nothin'. Let's go!"

Harlem grabbed his keys and we left.

I sat looking out the car window at how beautiful the sky was. Tamia's "Me Myself and I" filled the car and Tay was singing along. I won't lie—my feelings were hurt at how Harlem's mother treated me, but . . . for the first time in my life, everything was crystal clear. And all of this that I've been going through suddenly made sense. In order for my life to change, I had to act. I couldn't help but laugh as I wiped the tears rolling down my face.

This wasn't about being humiliated, this was about being free. Free of all the demons that haunted me: welfare, Quamir, his cheating, Shanice, shame, embarrassment . . . all of those things had a hold on me. But no more.

We pulled up in front of my house and Tay got out. She rolled her eyes at Harlem, and said, "Call me." She took her right fist and placed it in front of her eyes. "It ain't nothin' but a word."

"I'm alright." I laughed. "You can get in your car and go home now. I'll call you tomorrow."

"You sure?" she said, looking in my face.

"Yes, girl."

"Alright." She walked across the street to her car and got in.

I know she could tell that I wanted to cry, but there was no way I was going to break down in front of Harlem. I'd done so much groveling in front of men that I was determined to never do it again.

"Yo, listen." He sighed. "I hate that things turned out like this." He ran his hands through my hair. "I just—I just . . ." he said as if he were at a loss for words.

"No, it's okay—"

"No, it's not okay," he insisted. "My mother had no right to treat you like she did. I can't believe she went out like that. She's never done that before."

"Well, you've never dated a teenage welfare mom before," I snapped as I shot him a plastic smile. I knew it wasn't his fault, but at that moment it sure felt like it. "Listen—"

"No, look." He reached in his pocket. "You're special to me. And I know I haven't always acted the way I should've and we didn't start out on the best foot, but I'm here and I'm not going anywhere. Forget my mother. It's about me and you."

"Harlem—"

"Wait, Toi, please." His eyes pleaded with me. "I have something for you." He placed a small red box in my hand. For a moment, I looked at him like he was crazy. I know he didn't think that I was about to marry him, not after the day we just had.

"I know this is not a ring."

He laughed. "Nah, it's not that. But it means just as much, at least to me. Open it."

As more tears filled my eyes and threatened to spill out, I opened the box. "Oh my God, this is beautiful!" I pulled out a white gold chain with an eternity three heart pendant. The hearts were made of diamonds and they went from the largest heart on top to the smallest on the bottom. "Harlem, this is so beautiful."

"The hearts represent us, together. Me, you, and Noah."

"Listen—"

"Toi—"

"No, let me speak, please." I grabbed his hands and placed them between mine. "I have learned so much from you in the time we've been together. I've laughed, loved, and learned so much about myself. I've spent so much time trying to be somebody's chick that I didn't realize until now that love starts within. So," I handed him his necklace back, "I can't accept this."

"Why?"

"Because this is it, Harlem. I need some time to get to know me. I need to become a friend to myself and make things right for me and my son."

"And what—I can't be a part of that?"

"No, sweetie. You can't. I need to do this alone."

Harlem sat silently for a minute. I could tell by the way he was looking at me that a thousand thoughts were running through his mind.

"I need to do this."

"But I can't let you leave like that. We can work this out."

"Work what out, Harlem? I have a son and right now it's too much for you, for me, for us."

"Toi—"

"No, I have to be okay with this. This time I have to do this for me, otherwise I'll never change and things will always be the same. If it's meant to be, then I'll see you again."

"So you gon' bounce just like that?"

He had no idea how hard this was for me. "Yeah, Harlem. Just like that."

After a few moments he said, "Ai'ight, but I want you to have this." He reached around my neck and placed the necklace on me. "I want you to have this so you'll never forget me."

"How can I forget you?" I hugged him and placed my head on his chest.

"You know," he whispered into my hair, "that I loved you."

"And I loved you, too." I wiped my eyes and kissed him on the lips.

"You good, Pretty Girl?" he said as I got out the car.

I gave him half a smile. "Yeah, I'm good."

"Well, if you good then I'm good." He gave me half a smile back. "Just know I ain't gon' forget you though, ma, on May 20."

I was too busy fighting tears to pay attention to what the heck he was saying. I just wanted to walk away as quickly as I could. It was only a matter of seconds before I broke down. I knew this was the right thing to do, but dang, why did it feel so wrong?

21

___

"**B**roke down!" Cousin Shake yelled, scaring me out of my sleep. He banged on my bedroom door. "Don't sleep about it—be about it!"

"Retarded." Man-Man pounded on the door. "The slow bus is outside."

"Then you need to get on it!" I yelled from behind the closed door.

"What she say?" Cousin Shake snorted.

"Cousin Shake, she just cussed you out," Man-Man said in disbelief.

"Don't hold me back, jack, 'cause she must not know about me."

"She sleepin' on you."

"She don't want none of Cousin Shake. She . . . do . . . not . . . want none."

Oh . . . my . . . God . . .

"'Cause you know," Cousin Shake spat, "I will beat her like she stole my crack."

"You on crack, Cousin Shake?" Man-Man asked.

"Naw, I'm just sayin'."

"Oh, 'cause I was 'bout to say, Cousin Shake, you too old to be a crackhead."

I couldn't take it anymore, so I snatched my bedroom door open and popped my neck. "Bobby and Whitney, if you don't get away from my door!"

"Bobby and Whitney? Hold me back," Cousin Shake snapped, "'cause this chile here done lost her mind. Bobby and Whitney? Bobby and Superhead, yeah. But Whitney is far from being my type."

"Tell her, Shake!" I heard Ms. Minnie scream down the hall.

I'ma throw up.

Cousin Shake started skipping in place like a boxer . . . again. "You got the right one, bay-bay!"

"You . . ." he said slowly, "don't . . . want . . . none . . . of . . . Shake."

"I sure don't." I shook my shoulders in a dramatic shudder and said, "Now excuse me," and I slammed the door in his face.

I didn't have time to play with them. I had to get ready for the first day of school. I was a senior and I couldn't believe it. Finally, a senior . . . the year I'd waited for—only for me to still feel lost. And just when I thought breaking up with Harlem was the answer. Which obviously it wasn't because I was still in love with him and every time I thought about him my throat swelled with tears.

But, I had to get me together. And no, I didn't know where to start. I was having a hard time adjusting to all of this, this being responsible, being a mother, and somehow still being seventeen, but I had to get this right . . . otherwise, I was gon' bug.

I dressed in a pair of wide-leg Juicy jeans, a pink short sleeve tee with "Tantalizingly Fresh" in rhinestones across the breast, and pair of stilettos. Then I packed my backpack and my son's baby bag. I woke the baby up, dressed him, fed him and was out the door. Checking to make sure I'd placed bottles in his bag, I pushed Noah's stroller to the crowded bus stop, where people kept bumping into my baby's stroller and me.

"Excuse you!" I snapped at a group of kids.

"My fault," they said in unison.

"Dang." I sucked my teeth.

I looked at my watch. The bus was running late and I had to be on time for the first day of school.

After standing there for a few minutes with my book bag on one shoulder, the stroller in front of me and my feet aching in my high heels, I felt like a dressed-up bag lady.

Finally, the bus came and I was the first one to get on. As usual, the bus was crowded. People were sucking their teeth and getting aggravated with me because not only did I have all of this stuff, I had a big ole stroller to fold up. I slung my baby bag and backpack on one shoulder and held Noah in my right arm while trying to fold up the stupid stroller.

And wouldn't you know it, the damn stroller lock got stuck.

"Miss," the bus driver said, "you're holding up the line."

"I'm trying to hurry up." And as I said that, Noah started crying at the top of his lungs like I had dropped him or something. All I could do was take a deep breath and try it again.

"Let me help you, baby," the lady behind me said. "I'll hold him and you fold the stroller." She took Noah from my arms and I was able to fold the stroller and pay my fare.

"Thank you." I took my baby back.

As she passed me, I heard her say, "Don't make no sense. Babies having babies."

I felt like such a dummy. And just when I thought I was off to a new start today.

Once I got to the daycare and signed Noah in, the director stepped outside of her office door and signaled to me. "Miss McKnight, I need to see you, please."

"Can I finish unpacking him first?"

"No need. Now, may I see you, please?"

I pushed Noah's stroller into her office. "Yes." I glanced at the clock; I had five minutes before the bus that I needed to take to school was due to come.

"I'll make this quick," she said. "You have to

take Noah back with you. We haven't received authorization from the welfare program."

"What?"

"Yes, they said something about not receiving all of the paperwork back."

I stood there for a moment trying to think of what she was talking about and then it clicked. Earlier this summer, when I was at the welfare office, I never took the paperwork back. And even worse than that, I don't remember what I did with the paperwork. Damn, I was ruined.

"Can you just please keep him until the end of the day?" I asked.

"I'm sorry but I can't do that."

I felt like crying. I bit the inside of my lip as I turned toward the picture window and watched my bus ride by.

Instead of saying anything, I just turned around and left. I really was at a loss for what to do, so I got back on the bus and went downtown to the welfare office. I signed in and waited patiently. What else could I do, short of crawling under a rock and dying? I couldn't believe I was back there; it was like I was almost where I'd started. God, I had to get out of this situation. I couldn't live like this the rest of my life. Maybe I needed to fill out my application to Spelman. Maybe I needed to fill out a couple of college applications.

"Ms. McKnight." A caseworker that I didn't recognize had called my name. "Come to the back, please."

I walked over and she held out her hand. "Hi, I'm Mrs. Parker."

"What happened to Mrs. Robinson?"

"She quit."

"Oh."

"So what can I do for you?"

We walked into the small conference room where the welfare workers met individually with their clients.

"Earlier this summer I applied for a childcare program, but I forgot to bring the paperwork back."

"Which program?"

"The teen moms in school one."

"Oh, that deadline has passed."

"Mrs. Parker." Don't ask me why but I started to cry. "I have to get into this program because I have to go to school. You don't understand—I really need your help."

She handed me some Kleenex. "Don't cry. There are other programs."

I wiped my eyes. "Really?"

"Yes." She handed me a stack of paperwork. "This is a similar program, except you have to pay a hundred dollar co-pay a month. Can you afford that?"

I had no choice. "Yes."

"Okay, great. And if you sit here and fill out the paperwork, I'll call the daycare and see what we can arrange."

"Thank you." I gave her the daycare information and she left the room.

Noah was asleep, so it made completing the stack of paperwork much easier. I couldn't believe this lady was so nice to me. The other workers would never do this. After an hour passed, I was done with the paperwork and the caseworker had come back. "Ms. McKnight," she scanned the papers, "you're all set." She held her hand out and I accepted her gesture. "Good luck!"

"Thank you. That means a lot."

"You look like a smart girl. I know you'll make something of yourself."

That made my day—well until I got outside and it was raining and my feet ached like hell. Forget this, I called my mother.

"Ma."

"Toi, why aren't you in school? They just called here."

"Don't go off ma." I explained to her everything that had happened that morning. "Can you come and get me?"

"Of course."

I waited for my mother inside the lobby. When she pulled to the curb, she hopped out and helped me place Noah in the car. I knew for sure she was going to go off—she was way too calm on the phone.

"Say it, ma." I said. "I'm listening."

"Okay," she sighed. "I'm proud of you."

"What?" I snapped my neck toward her so fast, it's a wonder I didn't get whiplash. "Huh?"

"I am. You're growing up. You could've fallen

apart at that daycare, came home and done nothing about your situation, but you didn't. You han-
dled your business like a woman and I'm proud
of you."

"Yeah, but I had to have welfare to do it."

"No, you did it. You did what you had to do
and that's what counts. You have to start somewhere, Toi, and this is your beginning."

"You think so, ma?"

"I know so." She sniffed, as she'd gotten misty-
eyed. "Now, all you have to do is get you some
sneakers and take off those heels." She laughed.
"And you'll be fine."

She was soooooo right because my dogs were
cryin'.

"Now are you going home?"

"No," I said. "I know it's late, but I'm going to
school."

"Okay."

"I'll just explain what happened. It's ten o'clock
and I should be okay for the rest of the day."

My mother gave me the biggest hug in the world.
"My girl! My . . . girl!"

Maybe, this life won't be so bad after all. "Ma,
can you—"

"Yes, Toi."

"Yes Toi what?"

"I will keep Noah until tomorrow and you can
take him back to the daycare then."

"You think you know everything." I smiled.

"I do."

"Ma—"

"Wait a minute, baby," my mother said as she snapped her fingers. "This is my jam." It was Salt-N-Pepa's "Push It." "Ahhh, push it," she rapped, "push it real good."

"For real, ma," I said as she pulled in front of my school. "You can calm all that down."

"Girl, you don't know nothin' 'bout that," she said in a fake southern drawl, "Now goodbye and have a good day."

"Bye ma." As she pulled off, I could hear the music floating through the crack in the car window.

I'd just finished my homework and decided that I needed to fill out my college applications. Seven had completed hers over the summer so I was late getting started. I just hoped I wasn't too late. I walked over to my dresser, grabbed the applications and spread them on my bed. As I lay back on my pillow and read the instructions, my phone rang. I looked at the caller ID and saw that it was Quamir.

Here we go again . . .

"Yeah?" I answered.

"Wassup? What's good?"

"You got it."

"Ai'ight, ai'ight, so why don't you come see me?"

"Nope," I said, making a popping sound.

"What?"

"Now I'm funny?" I could hear that he was pissed. "I pour my heart out to you and you play me."

"Qua-Qua," I couldn't even finish, I was laughing so hard.

"Oh, it's cool. Be like that, Toi. Be like that!" And the next thing I knew, he hung up.

I lay back on my bed and screamed with laughter at the top of my lungs. I swear to you, this was the best day of my life!

22

Since this was our senior year, we planned a series of fun events to raise money for our prom. And the rule was that whatever the seniors planned to do, the juniors had to help out, too. So every Friday we held an activity meeting to discuss the upcoming event, which was Rep Your Hood night at Celebrity Roller Skating Rink. Meaning, whatever clique you were with, or whoever your homies were, y'all got together, set up a skating routine, and put it on blast for the world to see. So you guessed it: Seven, Tay, Shae, and me were a team.

The juniors and seniors were given forty-five minutes to meet and discuss what they had planned for the night. "Okay," Ms. Lawson, the guidance counselor said. "We need some volunteers to take pictures for the yearbook."

About four people, including Shae, raised their hands.

"Great," said Mr. Rogers, the assistant principal. "What else is there, Ms. Lawson?"

"The skate booth."

I volunteered for that.

"Okay, now we need two volunteers to run the concession stand." And wouldn't you know it, Tay and Percy raised their hands.

"I got this," Percy insisted. "Serving runs in my family."

"Never mind," Tay shouted.

"I don't think so, Ms. Johnson." Ms. Lawson said. "You've already volunteered. Besides, I think it'll be nice if you and Percy worked together."

"Yeah," Percy cleared his throat. "I'ma put her behind the stand, make her work that set, and when she act funny," Percy tossed his lips to the side, "I'ma say 'You just better have my money!'"

"Out!" Ms. Lawson yelled at Percy. "Out!"

"I was just playing."

"Somebody go get Ms. Minnie," Mr. Rogers said.

"I'm leaving," Percy waved his hands in defeat. "I'm leaving."

"Anyway, class," Ms. Lawson continued as Percy walked out. "The event is next Friday. I think it will be a lot of fun and since it's open to the community, I believe we'll make a lot of money. So, I believe we're done. Any questions?" She looked around for a moment. "Seeing there are none, you may go to lunch now." And we all bailed out.

Once my girls and I got our lunch and sat at an empty table, we started talking about our routine. "Toi," Shae said. "You know how to do the Souljah Boy?"

"Yeah, but I thought we were going to mix it up."

"With what?" Tay asked.

"With like the Walk It Out, Cupid, and the classic baby—"

"What's that?" Seven asked.

"The Pop-Lock-and-Drop It!"

"Hollah!" we said simultaneously and exchanged high-fives.

"Y'all know that's my boo's favorite thing to do," Tay said.

"You don't have a boo," I snapped at her.

"Oh dang, I could've sworn that Chris Brown was at my house this morning. Was I . . . dreaming again?"

I just looked at Tay. "Be quiet."

"Ill." She place her hands on her hips. "And what's with your attitude?"

I sucked my teeth. "I miss Harlem."

They all looked at me like I was crazy. "You the one." Tay waved her index finger. "Got all high and mighty and cussed er'body out—"

"Messed around," Seven interrupted, "and dumped ole boy—"

"And now you miss him?" Tay sighed. "Girl, please."

"But I had to," I insisted. "Things were falling

apart and I needed to do this for me. I needed to get myself together so that I wouldn't have any regrets about life."

"What . . ." Tay said slowly, "the . . . hell . . . was . . . that?" She took her index fingers and made them like a cross. "Stay away. Yo azz done turned into an after-school special."

Seven and Shae started to scream like they were frightened, then they broke out into laughter.

"Shut up." I had to laugh at myself. "You don't understand."

"We understand," Seven said, "that you need to chill. You're trying to make all of these changes but change doesn't happen overnight. Calm down. You just dumped Quamir for good, you had a good guy but he wasn't exactly ready to be with a girl with a baby, so it is. Call him. It's not against the law. And until then, chill. 'Cause if I hear one more time about you trying to get life right, I'ma scream."

I thought about what Seven said as I sat at the table, twisting my lips. Maybe I had gone to the extreme again, but here's the problem. Where the hell was the middle? While my crew carried on with what routine we were going to do, I flipped my cell phone open and figured, what the heck. I had nothing to lose. I dialed Harlem's number. Just as my heart stopped thundering in my chest, I heard the computerized operator say "The number you have reached . . . has been changed."

"Who you calling?" Shae asked.

"Nobody," I played my heartbreak off. "I was checking my bill balance, that's all." Before I could continue with the lie, the bell rang and it was time for class again.

As I stopped by my locker I heard someone say, "Yeah, that's the bitch." I knew it was Shanice—just when I thought I this week had gone off without a hitch, here comes the glitch. I sighed as I turned around and glimpsed Shanice and two of her girls watching me.

"We got a problem here?" I spat as the chick, Kellia, who stood next to me, quickly walked away. I figured I may as well get it poppin' before they thought they had the upper hand on me. I looked Shanice directly in the face. "You ain't been in school all week and now you come this afternoon tryna flex. Girl, beat it." And yeah, she said something, but whatever it was, it wasn't enough to make me stop walking to class.

I took my seat and, of course, the ghetto birds came trailing behind me. The teacher hadn't come in the room yet, so they took the opportunity and ran with it. "She think that she's so bad, but I got bad, 'cause she knows I'ma kick her ass."

I rolled my eyes to the ceiling. They could talk as much as they wanted, as long as don't nobody put their hands on me. Then I'd have to punch 'em dead in their face.

"Besides, she know that ain't Qua's baby."

As if it were an involuntary reaction, my back arched and I had to turn around.

"You got something to say to me?"

"No. What I heard is you screaming when I stomped you off your porch. And now all of a sudden you decide you don't have enough credits to get your G.E.D., so you come back to school, and you tryna rock with me. Girl, please. You better back up before you get smacked up."

"You just better leave my man alone."

"What man?" I spat. This whole deal with fighting over Quamir was ridiculous, especially since he was still sweatin' me and I didn't want him anymore. "You know yo azz a lesbian." I just threw that out there. Since she wanted to play dirty so bad, let's see if she could handle that. "Now sit yo dike behind down before you catch one."

Honestly, this was embarrassing, cussing out the very chick that when it got down to it, I had nothing against. Heck, Quamir didn't treat us any different, it's just that she obviously hadn't caught the hint. "Besides, he ain't shit. I don't want him. He got babies everywhere. You think we the only two with kids by him? Girl, please. Fall back and relax. Trust me, that dog will be back to piss on you. He hasn't gone far." I turned around in my seat and the next thing I knew the teacher walked in the room and was yelling at Shanice. "What are you doing, Ms. Jones! Out!"

I turned around and behind me was an official

uproar. Shanice was out of her seat, reaching for me.

"Toi, please come up here by me as Miss Jones leaves," the teacher said. I did as she asked, and a few seconds later Shanice walked out the room.

"Yo!" Tay called behind me after school as I headed for the bus stop. "Wait up." She jogged toward me. "What you rushing for?"

I turned around and started walking backwards. "I have to pick up Noah from daycare and if I'm late there's a charge."

"Alright." She caught up with me and I started walking forward again. "I'ma go with you."

"Where's your car?"

"It broke down."

"Oh, well come on."

The bus was coming as we headed toward the stop so we ended up having to run and hopped on. There was a crowd of kids from school on the bus, and I felt like most of them were talking about what happened between me and Shanice.

"You know me and Shanice had it," I said more as a statement than a question.

"What? When?"

"In biology class. She started kickin' all this ra-ra in the back of class, up there with Yaanah, Deeyah and them talking about me."

"Yo, she went south like that? Oh." She gave a sinister laugh. "I'ma see this chick."

"Forget her. I don't care what she does. I know

there's nothing between me and Quamir and if she doesn't, then, oh well. Not my issue."

Tay looked at me, surprised. "I can't believe this. You don't wanna see about her?"

"No, because she looks stupid still wanting to fight over Quamir. Please—he's no good and I'm done with the drama."

Tay placed the back of her left hand against my forehead. "Are you okay?"

"I'm fine." I laughed. "I'm just not fighting anymore. I'm good."

"Well hell, if you good, then I'm good. So anyway, did you see Katina?"

We laughed and gossiped about some of the chicks in our school as we rode to Noah's daycare. And once we got there, Noah was all ready to go. We gossiped even more on the way home. "Ai'ight, Tay," I said once we reached our stop. "I'll see you in the morning."

"Ai'ight, see you." And she disappeared down the street.

23

"Ma," I said to my mother as I lay across the foot of her bed watching TV. "Can I ask you something?"

"What?" She stood in the mirror putting makeup on.

"Do you ever like . . . question a decision that you've made?"

"A decision like what?" She puckered her lips and put her MAC lip gloss on.

"About . . . a guy."

"Uhmm." She slipped a tight black dress on. "Sometimes. Why? Because you miss Harlem?"

I sat up. "Is it that obvious?"

"Uhm hmm."

"So you think I'm dumb?"

"Do you?" She placed a pearl necklace on.

"Sometimes I do."

"Why?"

"Because I can't stop thinking about him and I just wanna hear his voice."

"Call him."

"I can't, his number was changed."

"Really?" she said, surprised. "Well, Toi . . ." she said as if she were thinking of something to say. "You know . . . you're young . . . and there will be a thousand boys. I just don't want you settling and making . . . some of the mistakes I've made. You have other things to think about, like school, college, your son. Harlem was a nice guy, but there are plenty of nice guys."

But I only want Harlem. "You think?"

"I know so." She turned away from the mirror and faced me. "How do I look?"

I looked her up and down in her form-fitting sleeveless black dress, chiffon shawl, pearl jewelry and stilettos. "You look beautiful. Where are you going?"

She threw her right shoulder forward and winked. "I have a date."

I hopped off the bed. "A date? And with who? Daddy's back in town?"

"No." She blushed. "I'm the only one who will call this one daddy."

"Ill, ma." I couldn't believe she said that. "Save the visuals, just tell me who he is. Did you tell Seven?"

"No, I was hoping she would be home from work so she could meet him."

"Oh, we get to meet him? Must be serious. So, who is he?"

"He's a train conductor. His name is Khalil. Well, Mr. Khalil to you."

"Ma." I looked at her with one eye closed. "You dating a dude named Khalil? You robbing the cradle ma?"

"Who you talking to?" she snapped.

"I just saying."

"Well don't say it like that, and no, he's older than me. In his forties, since you must know, and he's a nice guy." Before she could go on, the door bell rang.

"I'll get it."

"How do I look?" my mother repeated, seeming nervous.

"Beautiful."

"Okay, go get the door and I'll make a grand entrance."

As I went to open the door, Cousin Shake, Ms. Minnie, and Man-Man beat me to it. "Hi," said my mother's date, who was the spitting image of Denzel Washington. "I'm Khalil."

"Yeah," Cousin Shake opened the door and soon as Khalil walked in, Cousin Shake started frisking him.

"What are you doing?" Khalil frowned in shock. "Back up."

"Oh no you didn't," Ms. Minnie wiggled her neck. "Look like he tryna buck on you, Shake."

Cousin Shake started running in place. "You

tryna play me?" He backed up and then thrust into Khalil's face as if he were going to leap and then suddenly changed his mind.

"You must be Cousin Shake, you must be Ms. Minnie, and you must be Amir." Khalil chuckled a bit. "I've heard a lot about you, and it's nice to finally meet you."

"I bet it is." Cousin Shake sneered.

"Oh . . . kay." Khalil said. "So, can you tell Grier I'm here?"

"Why?" Cousin Shake looked him up and down. "You know you ain't gettin' no booty don't you?"

"He tryin' get some booty?" Man-Man started swinging punches in the air. "Do I need," Man-Man spat, "to unleash the secret weapon?"

"What secret weapon?" Ms. Minnie asked.

"Y'all need to cut it out," I said with my hands on my hips.

"You must be one of the twins." Khalil smiled at me.

"Yes, I'm Toi."

"Broke down!" Cousin Shake yelled at me. "Stay out of this."

"This grown-folk bidness!" Ms. Minnie insisted.

"Wow," Khalil shook his head. "You guys are really a lively bunch."

"What, you think they a circus act or something?" Ms. Minnie said, instigating. "What you think, they clowns?"

"Clowns?" Cousin Shake snapped.

I looked at Khalil and I couldn't tell if he

wanted to laugh, if he thought they were crazy, or both.

"You want me to go and get my mother?" I asked him. "She'll be out in a few minutes, though."

"It's cool," he said, amused. "I can wait."

"Is he tryna punk us, Cousin Shake?" Man-Man asked.

"Seems so," Cousin Shake insisted. "Seems so."

"So I need to unleash it, huh?"

"Lower . . . " Cousin Shake spoke slowly, "the boom."

"Ain't nothin' but a word." And don't you know, this fool scrunched up his face, contorted his body and let out the biggest fart in the world! And as if lightning had struck, Ms. Minnie immediately passed out.

I couldn't believe it. It was as if his behind opened up and growled. The fart was so loud that within an instant everyone started coughing and Cousin Shake started shaking like he was having an epileptic seizure.

"Mahhhhhhh!" I screamed and she came running into the room.

She placed her hand over her mouth and embarrassment covered her face. She pointed at Ms. Minnie. "Is she still alive?"

"I don't think so," I said. "I think your son killed her."

My mother looked around in shock. "Khalil, I'm so sorry." She sauntered over to Man-Man, who was now farting in a rumbling succession. He didn't even know my mother was behind him until she yanked him by his ear. They disappeared into the other room and when she returned, all I saw was a cloud of white smoke following her. "He should come to in about an hour."

"Alright," I said.

"Oh," she said to Khalil as she grabbed his hand. "I didn't introduce you. The trash compactor in the other room is my son, Amir. This here is my daughter, Toi. My other daughter, Seven, is at work. Ms. Minnie is the one passed out on the floor, and the one over there having a seizure," she pointed, "is Cousin Shake."

"We've met." Khalil smiled at us. "Are you ready, baby?" he said to my mother.

"I sure am," my mother said, a little too sexy for me. She winked and as she walked out the door she turned to me. "Don't wait up."

24

"Yuck!" Seven said. "Mommy really has a boo?"

"What's yuck about it? She has to live, too," I said as we dressed for Senior Night at Celebrity. I'd laid out a pair of Juicy jeans and an extra-tight tee with my name written in rhinestones across the breasts, and a pair of cute Juicy sneakers. My hair was styled in the natural waves that flowed to my shoulders and my lips glistened with clear lip gloss.

"But still." She slipped on her Roccawear sweat suit.

"Still what? I know you're not waiting for her to take Daddy back."

"No . . . but I guess I'm not ready for all of this moving on. I mean, suppose she really likes this dude. Then what?"

"Then what—what?" My mother came into my room and flopped down on the center of my bed.

"And what are you doing home?" I smiled at her.

"I have to babysit, remember?" She pointed to Noah's crib, where he was sleeping. "You guys look so cute. I hope you win the contest."

"Oh, don't sleep," I said. "We will definitely win."

"Soooooo," my mother said as if she'd been dying to ask. "What do you think of Khalil?"

"I don't like him," Seven spat.

"You don't even know him." My mother looked surprised.

"Well, I don't like the idea of him."

"And why not?" I asked.

"Because, like . . . what if he wants to move in here or be your husband or something. Then where does that leave us?"

"Homeless," my mother said sarcastically.

"Ma," Seven whined. "Be for real."

"Look, I know this is new to everyone, but it's time for me to live. There's more to me than just being mommy. Now, no one is coming in here and taking your place or anything else you may be thinking. But I like this man and I think he's nice and if you give him a chance you just may like him, too."

"Uhmm." Seven arched her eyebrows. "Oh . . . kay."

"Whatever, Seven." I shook my head as I looked at the clock. "It's time to go."

"If 'Push It' comes on," my mother yelled as we walked out the room, "be sure to dance for me!"

198

The bass from 50 Cent's "I Get Money" went straight from the DJ booth to the impatient line growing outside. It was Class of 2008's night and everybody was here to rep their hood. The music floated through the air, seducing anybody who was anybody and the who among who to rock this spot.

As I started taking tickets and giving out skates, I could hear Tay and Percy arguing. "I'ma slap you so hard," Tay spat, "you gon' grow!"

"Do it!" Percy dared her. "And by the time I get finished with you, you gon' be the same height as me!"

I couldn't help but laugh.

After an hour of servicing people, I called the guidance counselor and asked her to cover me so I could use the bathroom. Once I reached the bathroom, there was a line outside the door and it took me about five minutes just to make it in. I hurried in the stall, peed, and came back out. When I approached the sink to wash my hands, I saw Shanice. Oh God, not again. She hadn't been back to school since that day and I didn't feel like being bothered by the bull all over again.

"Toi—"

"Look," I cut her off. "I don't need the drama, and really, I'm not in the mood. There's nothing going on with Quamir and me. He doesn't come to see his son, so as far as I'm concerned, there is no Quamir, okay. So please don't start nothing and I won't have to finish it."

"First of all, chick," Shanice spat at me. "I wasn't gon' say nothing to you because Quamir is garbage and quite frankly, you can have him. He around here telling chicks that I'm crazy and shit. Psst, please forget him. So whatever problem you got with me, you can drop it because I am so not interested in entertaining you or your sorry ass baby daddy." And she stormed out the bathroom.

"Dang," was all I could say as I thought about what just happened. I couldn't help but laugh as I walked out the bathroom.

Seven, Shae, and Tay skated toward me, "Where have you been? The DJ's calling us to the floor. It's our turn to rep our hood."

"But what about my booth?"

"Forget that booth," Tay said.

"Yeah," Seven joined in. "The guidance counselor is over there."

"Exactly," Shae said. "Now come on."

"Oh, y'all just gon' ignore me?" the DJ blasted into the mic, while pointing at us. The more he spoke, the more the crowd came alive. Everybody in Celebrity loved a skating crew challenge, even if the prize was nothing but bragging rights for the night.

"Oh, they scared, y'all." The DJ playfully antagonized us, then he pointed to another clique that was there to rep their hood. "They think The Play Girls gon' kill 'em."

"Please," I said. "Let's just shut them down real quick and be on our way." Tay gave the DJ the signal and Soulja Boy's "Crank That (Soulja Boy)" started bumpin'.

We skated to the middle of the floor with me and Seven in the center and Tay and Shae on each side. My series of gold bangles clapped together while we did every hip-hop dance you could think of. The crowd was going wild and people were clapping like crazy.

Once we were done, we took a bow and returned to our assigned post. By the time the night ended, we'd won the skating challenge and 2008's Senior Night had been the best ever.

25

"I got accepted!" Seven came in the house screaming at the top of her lungs, waving a letter in my face. "Spelman, here I come!" She grabbed me and started dancing around. "We're going to Spelman—we're going to Spelman."

"You got in!" my mother started to scream. "Yes!"

"Did you get your letter?" Seven looked at me.

"No." I said, trying to hide my disappointment. "Besides, it's okay. I may not be able to go away anyway. So it's fine. I'm happy for you."

"Yours will be here soon," my mother said, trying to reassure me.

"Ma, it's okay. Besides, I have Noah. How would I go to school in Georgia anyway? So please. It's no sweat."

"Well, I was thinking—"

Seven cut her off. "You're not marrying Khalil, are you?"

"No," my mother said. "Just listen. You know I told you about my thoughts that we should move to Atlanta."

"Yeah," me and Seven said simultaneously.

"Well, not only did I get the transfer, but I also got offered a promotion."

"What?" I screamed. "Yes!"

"Yeah! Ma!" Seven was excited. "That's great. So we'll be moving to Atlanta."

"We'll be moving to Atlanta!"

"When?" I asked.

"When you finish school. Plus, I have to find us a house first."

"Ma, that's wonderful. Well, look." I smiled. "I'm going to bed now. I'll see you in the morning."

Don't ask me why, but I felt like a failure. Like I was never going to get out of the rut I was in. Besides, who was I fooling, thinking I would get into Spelman. My grades weren't the best last year, so it is what it is.

I slipped on mine and then Noah's pajamas, cut the light off, placed Noah in his crib and got in the bed, and closed my eyes. I did what I could to be happy for my sister, then fell asleep.

26

Life was funny. It had a way of picking up and then, without warning, slowing down. It took me a while to get adjusted to the fact that Harlem was gone forever and that all I had left was the here and now—whatever the hell that was. Everyone had received their acceptance letters to Spelman except me, so I decided that when I got to Atlanta I would go to community college. And yeah, I was pissed and a large part of me was hatin', but I guess it is what is and at least I'm honest about it.

It was Christmas break and I was working the restaurant without Tay tonight. Her mother had already started packing her things for college, so she asked if I would take over her shift and I agreed—what else was there to do?

After I completed my shift, I went home, gave

my son a bath, and then got in the bed. I didn't care that it was only seven-thirty.

"Broke down!" Cousin Shake yelled as he opened my door. "Here, some mail came for you." He tossed it onto my bed. I reached over to my nightstand and cut my lamp on. My eyes scanned the envelope for the sender's address and I saw an H. Simms, Atlanta GA . . . H. Simms? . . . Oh my God—Harlem. I opened the letter so fast, it's a wonder the envelope didn't give me paper cuts.

"Wassup Pretty Girl?" his letter read. I had to read that line again. "Wassup Pretty Girl? I hope you don't mind me writing this letter to say wassup to you. I started to call but then I didn't feel like you tossing me to the left and I'd rather hold on to the hope that we'll be together again. I know you may not believe it, but my mother felt really bad about what happened that day you came to our house. How are Noah and the rest of your family? Was hoping that I was still your prom date, but it is what it is. Hollah back! Love always, Harlem."

I held the letter to my chest as if my heartbeat would make Harlem appear. I wiped my eyes, pulled out a pen and paper and wrote him a letter back. "Harlem, I've missed you for what feels like forever. I thought that I would never hear from you again, and I was so excited when I got your letter that I didn't know what to do. I think about you every day and I don't know what else to say really other than I miss you. And I hope to see you soon. My prom date hasn't changed. And I still love you. Toi."

I was on cloud nine and for the first time in a long time, I closed my eyes and smiled as I drifted off to sleep.

27

"**W**ould you get your face together?" Tay said as I collected a tip off one of my tables. "We going to Hotlanta, baby! Hollah!"

"No, you're going to Hotlanta. I'm going to Atlanta to work, probably end up in some country-ass town on the outskirts in a trailer, working at Piggy Wiggy for the rest of my life."

"Did the real Toi leave and get replaced by a dumb one?"

"No, I'm just saying. I haven't gotten my acceptance letter and what makes it worse is that I already told you about the letter Harlem wrote me. I wrote him back, and got nothing in response. Not to mention the prom is in two weeks and then graduation—do you see where I'm going with this?"

"Yeah." She shook her head. "To hell and back—

you sound a hot mess." And she left me standing there. And I guess . . . maybe I did sound a hot mess, but hell, how would you feel? It's like the more I move ahead, the further back I fall. I thought for sure once I'd made up my mind to go that I would be accepted to college, but ha-ha, psyched my own mind. All I would be doing when we moved to Atlanta would be taking my misery on the road.

Whatever.

I finished my shift by serving the rest of my customers for the night, collected my tips, and headed home for another night of blah . . . blah . . . blah.

28

It was prom night and my entire house was excited. All of my relatives were there, including my daddy, who sat across from Khalil, who, by the way, my mother liked more and more by the day. They were now a full-fledged couple and I could tell that Tre McKnight didn't know what to do with himself.

Cousin Shake and Ms. Minnie had volunteered to be chaperones and, as always, they'd outdone themselves. Cousin Shake had on a sky blue tuxedo with a black stripe going down the side, a white shirt with ruffles going down the middle, about fifteen gold chains draped around his neck, and a crisp clean pair of sky blue L.A. Gears. And Ms. Minnie wore a red leather mini skirt, a white ruffled shirt, and leg warmers (and yeah, it was spring—May, to be exact). On her feet were a pair of clear jelly stilettos that lit up like Christmas lights every time she took a step. They were in the living room doing a bunch of jailhouse poses as Seven and I were in the back getting ready.

Although I tried not to show it, every time the bell rang I prayed that it was Harlem. But so far it had rung for what felt like a hundred times and it wasn't.

"I want you to do me a favor," my mother said as I sat on the edge of the bed and she put make-up on my face. "I don't want you thinking about anything that has gone wrong. All I want you to think about is what's right."

"Ma, I'm not depressed."

"I know, but I also know that you want certain things in life and they're not unfolding exactly the way you planned."

"My life is crazy." I tried to laugh, but I really, wanted to cry.

"No, it's not, Toi. It's life, and guess what? Shit happens. And when it does, you just start again. Now, you have been moping around here for too long with this long face. You're so busy concentrating on what isn't that you're missing what is. And what *is,* is you are a beautiful young lady, you're smart, you've become responsible, you take care of your son, you get good grades, and you've come a long way. I'm proud of you and starting tonight, I want you to be proud of you, too." She kissed me on my forehead.

"You ready?" Seven said, walking into my room, looking like a princess in a periwinkle cocktail dress that stopped at the knee and showcased her beautiful legs. Her hair was styled in a wreath of Shirley Temple curls.

"Oh," my mother said breathily (she was *so* dramatic). "You two look beautiful." She took us by the hands and we looked in the mirror, my mother in the center and my sister and I on the sides. "You two," she wiped her misty eyes, "look just like me!"

We looked at my mother and fell out laughing. She held our hands and we walked into the living room and everyone started snapping pictures. Josiah was there waiting for Seven and Tay was waiting for me. We decided we'd go together since neither one of us had dates.

Josiah and Seven rode together in a Mercedes Benz he'd rented for the night and Tay and I rented a stretch limousine.

I didn't think I would, but I was having a good time. I danced, ate, kicked it with my classmates, and Josiah and Seven were crowned Prom King and Queen. Although I tried to fight it, I looked for Harlem all night. I did force myself to have a good time, well, at least until the slow jams came on and Percy and Shim-daddy were grinning at me and Tay. Believe it or not, Cle'otis had a date.

"Wassup?" Percy was dressed in what looked to me the new millennium version of a Mighty Mouse outfit: a red velvet suit with a short royal blue cape and red and blue alligator shoes. "I know you wanna dance with a pimp."

"Not even . . ." I said, "if Jesus told me to do it." And I left him standing there.

"They crazy," I said to Tay.

And when she didn't respond, I turned around to see why not. You wouldn't believe this—this chick was over there dancing with Percy and Cle'otis. One in the front and one in the back . . . oh my . . . all I could do was laugh.

"Broke Down." Cousin Shake walked over to me. "Can I have this dance?"

"Aww, Cousin Shake. Of course." Cousin Shake held me by the waist and we swayed to an oldie but goodie, "No More Daddy's Little Girl." "I didn't get a chance to tell you," Cousin Shake whispered in my ear, "but you look beautiful tonight. I mean, your sister look alright, but you puttin' her to sleep. The only one who looks hotter than you is Minnie."

"Wow, Cousin Shake. What a compliment. Thank you."

"Ai'ight," he said as the DJ switched to the cha-cha slide. "Be up off me now. I gotta go Charlie Brown with my fifty-year-old tender." And he jetted.

I hunched my shoulders; hell, what did I have to lose? I went on and cha-cha'ed, too.

212   And by the time the night ended, I'd stopped thinking about everything that I expected to happen overnight and started just living and enjoying my life.

29

The morning of graduation, I stood in the mirror smiling at myself. Finally, I'd done what I set out to do. I ended the year with good grades and feeling like I would make it. I was determined to be all that I could despite being a teenage mother and people thinking the odds were stacked against me. I'd made it this far and now I was aiming for the stars.

"Look at my baby," my mother whined as she walked in my room. "I'm *soooo* proud of you."

"I'm so nervous, ma."

"Don't you be nervous." She picked up my cap and gown and helped me to put them on. "You are a beautiful young lady and I know that the sky is the limit." She placed my cap on my head. "I know that no matter what, you will get through it. All you have to do is put your mind to it."

She kissed me on the forehead. "I love you, ma," I said.

"I love you more."

"Alright now." My daddy pushed the door open. "Let's go. Cousin Shake wants to say a graduation prayer and then we'll be on our way."

"Oh no, ma." I looked at her. "You promised."

"I know, but you know how he is."

We walked into the living room where everyone was holding hands. My mother and I joined the circle and at Cousin Shake's insistence, we bowed our heads. "Hmmmm . . . " Cousin Shake began to pray. "We are gathered here today to say thank you. Thank you for upgrading Broke Down, for showing Fat Mama there's more to life than a sandwich, and for seeing this crew through to graduation. We about to take on a whole adventure and my Lord Jesus Crisco, you and I both know that Hotlanta will never be the same. Now, let's roll. Amen."

"Is it New Year's?" Seven asked.

Cousin Shake started running in place. "Believe me . . . you . . . do . . . not want none of Shake."

Everybody started laughing. My mother opened the front door and was laughing so hard that she bumped right into the mailman, causing the letters in his hand to scatter on the porch. I reached down to pick them up and the one on top was from Spelman. "Ma." I showed her the envelope as she said excuse me to the mailman for bumping into him.

"Open it," my family chanted, all staring at the envelope like it was gold.

"I can't," I said. "Suppose they said no?"

"Give it here," Cousin Shake said. "I'll open it." He tore the side of the envelope and slid the letter out. "Auh unnn," he cleared his throat while rattling the letter. "Dear Broke Down—"

"It doesn't say that," my mother snapped. "Now read it."

"Okay," he said. His gaze scanned the letter and then he started to read. "We know you been sweatin' us for months and we decided," he paused, and it felt like eternity, "that you need to stay yo ass home. Nah, it says pack your bags and come on to Spelman!"

My mother snatched it from his hand. "You got accepted!!!!" she screamed and we all started to do a dance. My sister held me so tight that she smushed Noah, who I held on my hip.

I couldn't believe it . . . I, Ms. Toi McKnight, was going to college!

Drama Part IV

No More Drama

30

August in Atlanta was nothing like it was in Jersey. Atlanta was hot, sweaty, and the extra bright sun made me feel like I was on a tropical island somewhere. Everything on campus seemed so foreign to me, from the old brick buildings to the cliques of sororities and fraternities, African flags flying, and all the clubs handing out pamphlets about getting to know your history and how to join their groups.

We were standing in line to register for classes and the campus was mad crowded with people from everywhere. For a moment, I felt like I was lost in a sea of students because I'd never seen so many people in my life.

Spelman's campus was huge and although it was all girls, there were cuties all over the place. We even had classes with the Morehouse cats.

"You know," Tay smacked her lips, "that I'ma join a fraternity." She looked around and pointed to a few boys dressed in shirts with Greek letters on them. "I'ma join all of them."

Me, Seven, and Shae looked at her like she was crazy. "You mean a sorority?" I laughed.

"No." She curled her top lip, and pointed to the clique of cuties with Q-dog shirts on. "I mean fraternities. Excuse me for a minute." She walked over to them and introduced herself.

"Toi," Seven said, "I forgot something in my dorm room. Come back with me, Shae."

"Alright, we'll catch you in a minute, Toi," Shae said as they disappeared.

Seven, Shae, and Tay all stayed on campus. I stayed home with my family, but that was cool—it was like I had the best of both worlds . . . well almost, because not a day went by that I didn't think about Harlem.

I reached in my bag and pulled out a list of the courses I needed to take.

"Yeah, girl," floated from behind me. "They call me Lil' Bootsy. How you doing?"

Oh . . . no . . .

"Don't you worry about how they doing," I heard Ms. Minnie say from behind me. I had no idea they were in Georgia . . . I shoulda known . . . I shoulda known . . . "You better worry," Ms. Minnie carried on, "about all this money I'm about to spend. About to have me walking the streets, catching the bus, wandering around trying to think of

ways to pay these people they money and you acting crazy. Better break yo self, fool."

Oh . . . my . . . God . . . All I could do was shake
my head. This was a hot ass mess. And just when I
thought they wouldn't notice me, Percy screamed
my name. "Toi Sharee McKnight, I been looking
all my life for you, girl."

I turned around slowly.

"Don't worry, Toi," Ms. Minnie said. "I'm regis-
tering his li'l ass in the slow classes."

Jesus.

"And don't get up here," Ms. Minnie went on,
"embarrassing me, talking about you tryna get on
the basketball team."

It took me about an hour to finally get to the
front of the line. I registered for my classes and
smiled as I walked away, looking at my schedule.
Then suddenly I felt like I'd just run into a brick
wall. My paper fell out of my hand and my backpack slipped off my shoulder.

"Watch out, Pretty Girl."

I looked up and it was as if the sun was shining
only on us. All of the people standing around us
disappeared and all I saw was Harlem standing
there. I pinched myself to see if this was a dream,
but when I felt the pain from the pinch I realized
it wasn't.

Harlem smiled. "Ma, look at you. You were
beautiful that last time I saw you but you've become even prettier."

"I never stopped thinking about you."

"Yeah?" He arched his eyebrows. "Well, how come I never got a response to my letter?"

"I wrote you back! I even waited for you the day of my prom."

"You did?" he smiled. "Well, I never got your letter, baby."

"I missed you sooooo much."

"Really? I got one better than that."

"What's that?"

"How about I never stopped loving you."

My heart started racing. I didn't know what to say, so I simply tucked my bottom lip into my mouth.

"You really still love me?"

He placed his arms around me. "You don't believe me?" He laughed, hugging me. "I promise you I still love you."

"How much?" I laughed, doing what I could to hold my corny ass tears back.

"This much." Then he yelled, "I love Toi McKnight! See this girl right here? In the last year, I never stopped thinking about her, and I never . . . ever . . . for one second, stopped loving her!"

"You can calm down," I said, tight-lipped, while looking at all the people staring at us.

"Nah, there's only one way to make me calm down," he said as he pressed his lips against mine.

"And what is that?" I responded to his kisses.

"If you be my girl again."

I stood there for a moment, looking into his

eyes. I thought that dreams didn't come true, but here I was, living a dream. He was beautiful and he wanted me and I wanted him and now I think I've grown enough to handle this. I've come a long way since fighting Shanice and chasing Quamir. I knew life was what I made it and I was determined that this go-round I wasn't settling for anything less than the best. "Yes," I said as he kissed me again. "I'ma always be your girl."

IF I WAS YOUR GIRL

Ni-Ni Simone

ABOUT THIS GUIDE

The following questions are intended to
enhance your group's reading of
IF I WAS YOUR GIRL.

Discussion Questions

1. In the beginning of the story, do you think Toi was wrong for showing up at Shanice's door? If it were you, would you have done the same thing? Why or why not?

2. Do you think Toi had low self-esteem?

3. Do you feel that Toi and Quamir loved each other? Do you know any couples like them?

4. Did you think that Harlem loved Toi? Why or why not?

5. Did you think that Harlem's mother was right in her thinking? Do you know anyone like her?

6. Do you think that Toi was a good mother? Why or why not?

7. Do you think that Quamir was a good father? Why or why not? Do you feel there was a big difference in Quamir and Toi's father?

8. What did you think of Seven no longer being a virgin?

9. Were you surprised that Toi went to college? Why or why not?

10. What do you think will happen now that the family has relocated to Atlanta?

A Chat with Ni-Ni Simone

What do you like most about being an author?

What I like most is that I can bring all of my dreams to life. If I want to be a singer, a dancer, or a rapper then I can be. The world on paper is limitless. But I couldn't do it without my education. And no, I'm not a walking afterschool special, but I do keep it real. I know I couldn't write books without paying attention in my English classes and when it came to the literary contracts, math was useful too—LOL.

What is one of the best things you've ever done?

Uhmmm, okay, dump a boy who didn't treat me like a lady. I had to let him know he had me twisted.

Name one of the worst things you've ever done?
Date a boy I didn't like.

Who is your favorite rapper?

You know it's Bow Wow.

Who is your favorite famous couple?

Beyoncé and Jay-Z, they are so hot!

What's your favorite TV show?

Actually, I have two: *Run's House* and Keyshia Cole's reality show *The Way It Is*. Oh, and *Flavor of Love*. Wait, wait, oh yeah, B,E,T,'s *Hell Date*. *I Love New York* is the bomb, too. And I do have two oldies but goodies, *Good Times* and *Little House on the Prairie*. What, chile please can you say J.J. and Nellie Olesen? I know that was more than two.

Want more?

Check out Seven McKnight's story,
SHORTIE LIKE MINE.

Available now wherever books are sold.

1

I ain't even gonna front . . .
Since you walked up in the club
I've been giving you the eye . . .
Must be a full moon . . .

—BRANDY, "FULL MOON"

It was official: I was fly. I had on my freakum
dress and the fat version of Lil Wayne was stalking me. Everywhere I looked, there he was. Grinning. As if somebody here in Newark, New Jersey
told him he was cute. He had drops of sweat running from his temples to his chin and was breathing like he was having an asthma attack. I was
embarrassed. Out of all the tenders lined up outside the club, hugged up on their honeys, and
kicking it with their boys, here I was being ha-
rassed by a baby gorilla in a short set.

My girls and I were in line, waiting to get in to
Club Arena for teen night, and for the first time in
my life, I was appreciating my size fourteen brick-
house hips. My hair was done in a cute ponytail,
swinging to the side with a swoop bang in the

front, my MAC was poppin', and my stilettos were workin' it out.

I resembled a voluptuous New New from *ATL*: two deep dimples, honey-glazed skin, full lips, and dark brown eyes shaped like a lost reindeer's. My sleeveless House of Dereon dress was the color of new money and the belt wrapped around my waist was metallic silver. My colorful bangles and big hoop earrings were courtesy of Claire's and the rose tattoo on my left calf was by way of the 99 Cent Store and warm water. So, you get the picture? Fierce was written all over me. And just when I started feeling comfortable with being the biggest one in my all-girl clique, tragedy struck . . .

"Yo, Shawtie!" my stalker screamed as if he were working at the Waffle House, making a public service announcement. He was standing at the door talking to one of the bouncers, when my friend Deeyah walked up and stood beside me. "Yo, Shawtie," he called again. "Deeyah"—he raised his arm in the air as if he were making a three-point play—"that's me right there."

My girls and I all looked around. We ain't know who the *heck* he was talking about.

"Seven, there go your new boo." Deeyah blew a pink bubble and popped it. "The one and only Melvin. Told you I was gon' hook you up."

Melvin? I tugged Deeyah on her arm. "Is this a joke?"

"What's wrong with him?" she snapped, rolling her eyes. "You tryna talk about my taste?"

Oh . . . my . . . God . . . I'ma die. "He looks like my sixty-year-old Cousin Shake."

"Everything is not about looks, Seven. When are you gon' to grow up and learn that?"

"When I'm done with being sixteen, which is not today. I don't believe this."

"Well, who did you think you were gon' get?" She popped her gum and smiled. "After all, Josiah is mine and the rest of his crew, well . . . I hooked them up," she said as she pointed at each of our friends: Ki-Ki, Yaanah, and Shae.

Ki-Ki and Yaanah shot me a snide grin as if to say, *That's right!* But Shae rolled her eyes and said, "Please, Deeyah. You lucky I ain't punch you in the face for that. Gon' hook me up with somebody named Shamu."

"Shamu is a nice name." Deeyah jerked her neck.

"But he followed me around in school." Shae sighed. "From class to class, and then I come to find out he was the oldest kid in special ed."

"Special ed?" Deeyah pointed to her chest. "He's in my class. So what you tryna say, Shae? So what if he wears a helmet? He needs love, too."

A helmet?

"Why"—Shae looked toward the sky—"do I even go through this?"

"Go through what?" Deeyah smirked. "Why don't you think about the future, Shae? Don't you know people in special ed get a check every month? Never mind, Shae. You just played yourself." She turned her attention back to me. "Seven, I know you got more sense than this chick, so you know you need a man that you gon' complement. Trust me. See Josiah, needs a chick like me. I'm a dime and you're a quarter. Josiah is the captain of the basketball team and Melvin over there"—she pointed—"is the team. Make sense?"

We all looked at Deeyah like she was stupid. "Can you say dumb-dumb?" I shook my head. "You so busy tryna dis me that you actually just gave me and ole boy over there a compliment."

"Girl, please. That flew over your head," Deeyah snapped. "You just played yourself."

"Deeyah, you just said you were a dime and she was a quarter." Shae sighed. "Get a clue."

"I could get a clue if I could stop passing it to you." Deeyah rolled her eyes. "Y'all so stupid. I'm tired of being the mother of this played-out group. Anyway, Seven, I called myself doing you a favor."

"A favor?"

"Yeah, I'm tryna save you from being played."

"Excuse you?" I could've smacked her.

"Think of it this way. If a guy is too fly, he might leave you for a skinny chick." She ran her hands along the sides of her body. "And with Rick Ross over there"—she snickered—"you ain't got to worry 'bout that."

Before I could decide if I wanted to body her or simply cuss her out, I felt a tap on my shoulder and hot breath on my neck. "What's good, Shawtie?" It was Melvin, looking me up and down as if he could take a biscuit and sop me up with his eyes. "I knew I'd seen you before—good look, Deeyah."

"You've seen me?" *I don't think I've been to hell yet.*

"Yeah, I pass you every day on my way to English class."

"Really?" I was beyond disgusted.

"Come on, Shawtie, ain't you in them honors classes? You real smart and er'thang." He had the biggest grin I'd ever seen. "My pot'nahs call me Big Country. But my name is Melvin. I just moved here from Murfreesboro."

"Murphy who?"

"Carolina, Shawtie." His gold tooth was gleaming. "You know, I-95 in the house, the dirty-dirty baby."

I was speechless. Not only was he fat, he was country.

"Speechless, huh? You ain't never seen nobody reppin' for the dirty-dirty like me befo'." As if he had a bullhorn and was doing the lean-back, he cupped each hand on the sides of his mouth and shouted, "MUR . . . FREES . . . BORO!!!"

God must hate me.

"I know you feelin' me, Shawtie." He grabbed me by the arm and pulled me toward him. "Gurl, you so sharp, you hurtin' me. Now, let's get on in here. You ain't got to wait in no line. We just gon' walk on in this piece. Now ya gurls, I can't do nothin' for them. Big Country's pull is limited."

"Oh, it's okay." I shook my head. "Really, it is. I'll just wait with them. You go on."

"Sab, Shawtie." He pinched my cheek. "I was just playin'. Psyched yo' mind." He ran his index finger across my forehead. "Y'all get on here and come on in this piece. Deeyah and Shawtie, y'all hold arms and y'all other two walk in front of me and let them know Big Country has arrived."

"That's all you, Melvin?" someone shouted as we walked in.

"All day playboy," he shouted back. "All day."

Jesus please . . .

As soon as we walked in, the bass in the music sent vibrations through the floor. The DJ was doing his thang—Baby Huey's "Pop, Lock, and Drop It" was playing and instantly, everyone, including Melvin, started dancing. I stood leaning from one foot to the other, wondering what punishment I faced next.

And just when I decided I should find a rock to climb under, Melvin threw his hands in the air and screamed, "This my jam right here!!" "Walk It Out" started playing and Melvin took to the floor again.

After the song finished, Melvin bought me a drink and dragged me to take a few Polaroids with him. In the midst of him squattin', leanin', and showcasin' a few jailhouse poses with me standing completely still, Josiah, Deeyah's boyfriend and number twenty-three on the school's basketball team, swaggered over with an entourage of his teammates. Two things about Josiah and his crew is that they were the finest in school and all the girls wanted them. But me, I only had eyes for Josiah and when I found out Deeyah was dating him, I think I passed out everyday for a week straight. She must've stolen him out of my dreams because that's the only way I could see me allowing her to walk away with him. Other than that, we woulda been throwin'. Please believe dat. But since I didn't think I had a real chance of him liking me, I stepped to the side and have been diggin' him from afar.

Josiah had a super-sized Uptown in his hand. He shook the ice, handed the cup to Deeyah, and she finished it off. Then he stood behind her with his fingers locked around her waist, his chin on top of her head, and he started staring at me.

Chris Brown's "Shortie Like Mine" was playing and for a moment I could swear Josiah's eyes were singing the lyrics to me. This made me want him even more. The crush I had on him was unshakable. He was not only the most wanted man in school, he was the best looking. He was so beautiful I was tempted to call him pretty. He superseded fine and gorgeous couldn't touch him. He was the type of dude that should've been a poster child for irresistible. Most people said he favored the rapper Nelly, but personally, I thought he put Nelly to sleep. He was so fine it didn't make sense. He was at least six feet, with skin the color of caramel in its richest form, the sexiest almond-shaped eyes in the world, and a fresh Caesar with brushed-in waves. His gear was always dapper: baggy jeans, an oversize skull belt buckle, a fitted black tee that read "I am Hip-Hop," and throwback Pumas.

"Can't speak, Seven?" he asked.

I know he had to hear my heart beating. "No," I snapped, and as an extra twist, I rolled my eyes.

"Yo, Josiah," Melvin interrupted. "Back up off me now. You know this is me right here."

"Yo, my fault, son." He smiled. "Do you."

"Whew, Shawtie," Melvin said, dapping sweat like a church lady in heat. "Give ya boo a sip of that soda."

Oh, he had me messed up. There was no way we'd reached the level of drinking after one another. "You see the bar over there." I pointed. "Go fetch yo'self one."

"Fetch?" Josiah snapped. "He ain't a dog."

"Is that why you responded?" I asked.

"You tryna say I'ma dog?"

"I'm tryna say you all up in here wit' it." I waived my hand under my chin as if I were slicing it.

"Dang, Shawtie, you just angry, huh?" Melvin said. "What, you PMS 'n or somethin'? Somebody hook my girl up with some Midol."

His girl?

"Now, Shawtie," Melvin went on, "act right in front of company and gimme some of that soda." He snatched the cup from my hand and I snatched it back, causing it to spill and splatter all over my dress.

"What, are you *stupid?!*" I couldn't believe this. "Oh, my God, you ruined my dress! You just dumb! Who invented you? Dang, you . . . get . . . on . . . my . . . nerves! Why don't you take I-95 and ride you and yo' gold tooth back down south. Uggggg! What crime did I commit to get hooked up with you?!" I hated being so mean, but didn't he ask for it? Looking at Melvin, I could tell I hurt his feelings because for the first time tonight he was silent.

241

"Yo," Josiah snapped, releasing his hands from around Deeyah's waist and standing up straight. "I think you owe my man an apology."

"Apology? If anything, you need to apologize for being up in my business!" I shouted. "Ain't nobody talkin' to you!"

"You know what?" Josiah said with extreme bass in his voice. "You gotta nasty attitude. And I really don't know what it's for, 'cause you look ridiculous, rockin' a buncha knockoff. If you so miserable, why don't you take ya fat ass home!"

Every tear I had in my body filled my mouth, which is why I couldn't speak. Yaanah and Ki-Ki were looking around the club as if they hadn't heard anything. When I looked at Deeyah, she'd covered her lips with her right hand and a snide smile was sneaking out the side. Shae was standing there in disbelief, looking at Josiah as if at any moment she was about to give it to him. "You know I got yo' back," she said.

I wanted to cry so badly, but I'd been played out enough and if I let this slide, then all of them

SHORTIE LIKE MINE

standing here would think they had the upper hand. So, this is what I did—I blacked on all of 'em. Straight up, I was 'bout to read 'em. "Deeyah, Yaanah, and Ki-Ki, I know y'all ain't laughin'." I looked at Shae for confirmation. "Should I get 'em, gurl?"

"Get 'em, gurl, 'cause I'ma get ole boy over here when you done." She placed her hand on her right hip and looked toward Josiah.

I snapped my neck. "Let me set you on fire real quick. We 'spose to be homegirls and y'all standin' here laughin', when everybody here know you three are the queens of knock off. If it wasn't for y'all, the Ten-Dollar Store woulda been closed down! You Payless-Target-Wal-Mart-havin'-Salvation Army freaks. Look like you get ya clothes out the Red Cross box. And word is, Josiah, you buy all of Deeyah's gear, so what that make you?"

"A hot-ass mess." Shae rolled her eyes in delight. "Looks like you been shut down, Superman."

"Whew, look at you girl," Melvin said, looking at Shae. "I likes me some aggressive women. Maybe I oughta hollar at you. What's your name?"

"Boy, please," Shae said.

Josiah shot me a snide smile. "Your mouth is ridiculous." He eyed Deeyah and the expression on his face seemed to dance in laughter. "Y'all shot out."

"I don't believe you went there, Seven," Deeyah said. "You know Ki-Ki ain't boostin' from the Red Cross box no more."

"Don't be tryna call me out!" Ki-Ki shouted. "That was Yaanah's idea anyway."

"Oh, no, you didn't . . . !"

And the next thing I knew, these three were in a brawl over whose idea it was to jack the donation-clothing bin. But hmph, I didn't care. What difference did it make to me when I felt like the whole club was still trippin' off how bad Josiah played me. I knew it was time for me to roll, I just didn't want it to seem like I was running from something, or better yet, someone. "I'm not beat for this." I managed to keep the tears that flooded my mouth at bay. I turned to Melvin. "My fault if I hurt your feelings."

"Oh, you ain't hurt my feelings, Shawtie. That just turned me on."

If I didn't feel like crying, I would've laughed. "I'm 'bout to bounce."

"Hold up, Seven," Shae called behind me. "'Cause I'm 'bout to bounce with you."

And just like *America's Next Top Model*, we threw our right shoulders forward, our bootylicious oceans in motion and proceeded out the door.

Stay tuned for
A GIRL LIKE ME.

Available in December 2008
wherever books are sold.
Until then,
enjoy the following excerpt.

SPIN

Track 1

Okay God, check it. I know that I prayed for my boyfriend, but it's time to renegotiate. I wanna new boo. And not any ole kinda boo, but a Hot Boy. Pants saggin' and timbs draggin'. A Young Buck or a Haneef type boo—one who—

"Elite," my eight year old sister, Aniya, whispered to me as she lifted her head from under the covers. "Can you tell God I wanna boo, too. But I wanna Patrick from Sponge Bob-type boo."

"Patrick?" Aniya's fraternal twin, Sydney, peeked her head from under the covers and said, "He doesn't even have on underwear."

"Well, you shouldn't be lookin'!" Aniya snapped, getting offended. "You too grown!"

Sydney held her hand up mid-way to her face. "You better talk to the hand 'cause the face don't understand."

"Oh, you got me twisted!"

"Alright!" I snapped, and they quickly retreated back under the covers.

In case you haven't noticed, late at night when the sun sets and the moon is just right, I like to pretend the ghetto twins don't exist. It's a little difficult considering we not only share the same room, but they sleep at the foot of my bed.

Which is why I make them go to sleep at least an hour before me, so I can have time to think. Otherwise, when would I find time to get my famous boo fantasy on? Sounds crazy, right? But not to me. That's why I've been waiting for ten o'clock (I've got an hour to go) to enter the sing for front row seats and a chance to be on stage with the hottest-hip-hop-and-R&B-sensation-Haneef radio contest.

Understand this—real talk, Haneef is putting Usher, Chris Brown, Bow Wow, and Omarion to sleep. Well . . . maybe not Chris Brown . . . 'cause he is kinda fly, but still—you get the point. Li'l daddy is doin' it: six feet even, Hershey's milk chocolate skin, beautiful, almond-shaped brown eyes, tight and tumbling muscles that go on into infinity, and a killah swagger like Jay-Z.

Haneef is that even-when-you-see-it, you still don't believe it type fine . . . and I swear, every time he's on the radio, he's singing not only about me, but to me. So please . . . don't hate.

My best friend Naja thinks I'm crazy. Whatever.

'Cause I never said a word when she was drooling over Flava Flav.

I look at the clock. Half hour to go. Let me call Naja so we can practice. As I reach for my Boost mobile, it dances in my hand.

It's Naja. Did I mention she pops her gum before every sentence? "I've been staring at the clock," she pops, "for five hours and it's movin' slow as hell."

"Are the batteries dying?"

"I think so. The number on the left stays the same for like an hour. And I'm like 'okay, you wanna move yo ass?'" She pops her gum again.

I never said she wasn't an air-head, I just said she was my best friend. Naja and I have been down like four flat since kindergarten.

I don't even comment on the clock thing. "First of all, you better fall back from my baby daddy, Haneef. You claimed Flava Flav."

"Ill, I don't want him anymore, but I do think Bobby Brown is kinda cute."

I made hurling motions with throat and neck. "I'ma throw up."

"You better take something, 'cause if you throw up on the phone and it flies over here . . . then we gon' have a problem."

"How would it fly over there? Know what—never mind."

"The clock moved!" Naja yelled, excited. "It's ten!"

A GIRL LIKE ME

I screamed, "Okay, okay. What we gon' sing?"

"Sing?" Aniya popped her head from under the covers again. "Whatcha-whatcha-know 'bout me . . . "

I ball my fist up and say, "If you don't shut your mouth."

"Puleeze," Sydney pops her eyes wide and rolls her neck. "She don't wanna sing that mess, she wanna sing, 'let me take you to bed, lead you to places you've never been.'"

"What in the—let me find out that you been singing that mess and see what happens to you," I threaten. "Now don't let me see you pop up from the covers again."

"I'm tired of being treated like a slave." Sydney sighs.

"Be quiet!" I yell.

"Come on," Naja snaps. "We have to hurry up. We should sing," she hesitates, "a Whitney Houston throwback. Hit all the high notes."

"Yeah, and get hung up on."

"I can sing," Naja said, certain of herself. "I put Rihanna to sleep."

"Wow, that's a hard thing to do," I said sarcastically. "Look, we don't have time to argue. I'll sing, you just hum . . . softly."

We called the radio station at least a hundred times before we were able to get through.

"Hot 102," the DJ said. "You're on live. Who is this?"

"Ahhhhhh!!!!!!!!" Naja screamed . . . in everybody's ear.

I swear, if we get hung up on, I'ma take her drawstring weave and sling her ass! "Would you shut up?"

"Ladies," the DJ said, getting our attention. "This is Hot 102 and you're live on the air . . ."

"Hey," I said. "My name is Elite and I'm from—"

"Brick City, in the house!" Naja cut me off. "I'm Naja and I wanna give a shout out . . ." I could hear her ruffling paper in the background, "to my mother at work right now, my brother on lock down, and to all the homies who ain't here—"

Oh my God! "Naja—"

"Wait," she carried on, "and to Al-Terik. You know I'm through with you 'cause I saw you and big butt Belinda in the corner of the cafeteria—"

"Naja!"

"Dang girl, you rude."

"We're supposed to be singing."

"Okay, and what's the problem? Sing."

"Thank you. Sorry about that, uhm, I wrote a song that I would like to sing—"

"Elite, they don't wanna hear no poetry."

I ignored her. "Okay, here goes. Do you want me to sing now?"

No answer.

I look at the phone to make sure it was still on and it was. "Hello?" My heart dropped in my chest.

No answer.

"Did they hang up?" Naja gasped.

"I think so." I couldn't believe this. "Hello?"

"Girl, they're gone. Dang, why would they do that?"

"I didn't even answer; I simply hung up on her, turned on my side and placed the covers over my head. I'm not surprised it didn't work out. Besides, my mother is a crackhead and the furthest I'll probably get in life is from one side of this tight ass bed to the other. Tears slide down my cheeks as I close my eyes and drift to sleep.

SPIN

Track 2

"**G**ood morning, welcome to Hot 102," the alarm clock radio echoed through my room, a signal that I needed to get up and get ready for school. I turned over on my back and stared at the ceiling, where my taped poster of Haneef flapped in the top left corner and sagged in the middle.

"We're here today," the radio continued, "with hip-hop sensation Haneef."

"Wassup, everybody!" Haneef said, and my heart palpitated.

"So," the DJ spat, filled with excitement. "Today is the last day to win tickets to the Haneef concert! So, if you can sing, give me a ring!"

Okay God, You must be trying to tell me something. I reached for the house phone and dialed the radio station with a quickness. And oh my

God . . . oh . . . my God, they answered on the first ring.

"Hot 102, who do we have on the line?"

"Elite!"

"Say hello to Haneef."

"I can't," I said in a pant. "I'm speechless."

I can hear Haneef laugh . . . and oh, what a beautiful laugh.

"Alright," the DJ continued on, "so you're calling for the contest?"

"Yes."

"Can you sing?"

"What? Boy, don't play with me," I said seriously. "Can I sing? I sing all the time, listen," and I burst out into the best soprano version of, "hahhhh . . . llelujah! Hahhhh . . . llelujah! Hallelujah, hallelujah . . . hah—lay-lu-yaaaaaa!"

"Oh . . . .kay . . ." the DJ said. "I hope that's not what you're going to sing for us."

"Oh no, my song is 'When You Touch Me.' It's a dedication to Haneef."

I close my eyes, open my mouth wide and Heaven springs from my throat. I'm naturally an alto with a sultry voice like Keyshia Cole, but I have a range like Mariah Carey, so there's no mistake that I'm straight killin' this contest! ". . . I'm missing you baby . . ."

"Lee-Lee!"

Hmph, I keep singing but I could've sworn I heard my mother just call me by the nickname she gave me. I glance at the clock and knew it wasn't her, because at this time of the morning, she's sleeping off her high from the night before. I close my eyes and continue.

". . . . miss when you touch me . . ."

"Lee-Lee!"

My eyes pop wide open. That is my mother.

"Elite Juliana Parker, get yo fresh ass off that phone talkin' crazy!"

Oh no! "Ma, get off the phone! I'm doing this to win tickets for Haneef!"

"Haneef? Who the hell is Haneef, some li'l hoodlum ass drug dealer? All you can do for Haneef right now is get his chin checked. You up here singing like you hot in the ass, about somebody touching you! Keep on singing and it's gon' be me reaching out to touch that ass! If anything, you need to ask Haneef if he got two dollars I can borrow. If not, then get yo ass off my line!"

Something tells me . . . I just died. I hang up the phone, lay back on my bed and my Haneef poster falls straight on my head.

A half hour into gettin' my misery on, I rise from the floor, shower and dress in a pair of fitted Juicy jeans, a matching V-neck tee, colorful bangles, and matching earrings.

When I walk in the living room, I see that either my mother found two dollars to borrow or she stole something to supplement it because she's not there. I promise you, Cassie Parker is a hot-blazed-up-mess.

She raised us from behind the bathroom door most of our lives because that's where she hid to get high. Like we really didn't know what was going on. But ever since she got with her new zooted-up boyfriend, Gary, they've taken crack love to the streets. Most of the time she's either in somebody's hallway, street corner, or abandoned building.

I've never had the type of home where my friends came over and kicked it in my room. As a matter of fact, the only friend who knows the real life that I live is Naja. Everybody else knows nothing. And I wanna keep it that way. The last thing I need is a buncha chicks or the state in my business. I've adjusted to being the "real" mother around here and it's cool. I love my sisters and brothers and whatever it takes to keep my family together is what I'ma do.

I would tell you about my father, but what would be the point? The shit is so typical that you'll probably ask me to be quiet mid-way through my explanation of why my biological seems to be confused between loving me and loving ole girl (my mother).

Needless to say, I'm nothing special. There are a thousand girls like me. This is just my story. So . . . it is what it is, and other than being played (twice) like too sweet Kool-Aid for Haneef tickets, I don't complain. What's the use? Have you ever known shit to change because you complained? Exactly. Which is why we keeps it movin' around here.

I walk over to the pull-out couch where my brother, Ny'eem, is asleep and say, "Get yo ass up!"

He sucks his teeth and ruffles the sheets, but do I look fazed. Puleeze!

"And don't think," I carried on, "that I don't know what time you came up in here last night. Play with me if you want to and you'll be down at the men's shelter or juvie somewhere."

"Shut up!" he snaps and stretches. "You always tryna be somebody's mother."

"I'm the best mother you got."

"What?" He stands from the couch and looks down in my face. He's only fifteen but he towers at least three inches over me. "Girl, I'm grown."

Grown? Did he just say he was grown? Is this suckah tryna buck? Okay, I see where this is going. I stand up on a rusted metal chair that somehow ended up as a part of our décor, and strike a karate pose, lifting my leg up high enough so that if I wanted to I could take it to his chest.

And don't you know he cracked up laughing so hard that tears fell from his eyes.

"You think I'm funny? Do I look like I'm laughing to you?"

"No, you look like you lost your mind." And he left me standing there.

"You just get ready for school!" I yelled behind him. "And let me hear you been skipping class again and see what I really do to you."

Just as I step down from the chair, my five year old brother, Mica, rushes out the bathroom with a sheet wrapped around his neck like he and super-man are boys. "What the hell? Boy, where are your school clothes?"

"I'm not wearing that shit!"

"Hol' up . . . hol' up . . . did he just cuss again!" I ball up my fist. See, Mica, he's the one I really have to bring it to, 'cause he think he's tough. But if I look at him hard and long enough, he'll burst out in tears. "Go put on those clothes. As much money as I paid that booster! I work at the mall part time—"

"Mommy gets a welfare check."

"And mommy gettin' high, too," Ny'eem snaps as he gathers his clothes for the day.

"Shut up!" I said to Ny'eem. "Now," I turned my attention back to Mica, "why don't you want to wear what I laid out for you?"

"Because I want my pants to droop down like Ny'eem's. You got a belt laid out for me, some hard bottom shoes, and a turtle neck. I may as well be going to church."

"I didn't lay a turtle neck out for you. It's a Phat Farm shirt. Know what? I don't have to argue with you." I stare him down and just like I predicted, he's in tears.

"Everybody treats me like a baby around here." He storms back into the bathroom.

Whatever, I go in my room where the twins have to be watched closely when they put on their gear because believe me, they will walk outta here draped in my Bebe, Baby Phat, and any other designer dig I either worked or got a hook up for.

And yes, they look a hot mess, considering I'm 5'5 and a size ten and they're just eight years old. So, I stand guard while they slip on their jeans, a cute li'l Bobby Jack shirt and some pink and white kicks.

Their hair is shoulder length and easy to maintain because for ten dollars, every other week, the girl across the hall puts in cornrows and beads. An hour after me acting like Jerome the flashlight cop, everybody is ready to roll.

As soon as the city bus doors open and I step foot in front of the school, I know right away that everyone here heard me get played on the radio. Especially since they all look at me and either smile too wide or laugh in my face.

But it's all good 'cause I will read these ghetto birds like they stole somethin'. Besides, don't get it twisted, just because I have a jacked-up home life doesn't mean I'm not fly—because I am. Honey colored skin, flat ironed straight hair that drapes past my shoulders, Asian eyes, full lips, thick hips, and a cover-girl smile.

Just as my Boost mobile vibrates through my purse, I see Naja running toward me. I twist my MAC covered lips and ignore her. Yes, I'm still pissed.

I flip my phone open. "Who dis?"

"Elite?" It was a male voice.

"Yeah."

"Wassup girl?"

"Terrance? Boy, didn't I tell you to lose yourself?"

"This isn't Terrance. This is DJ Twan from Hot 102."

"Yeah, right."

"Didn't you call us this morning for the singing contest?"

"Oh now you got jokes, Terrance? Look, I'm down to my last twenty minues on my phone, so I don't have time to waste with you on my line. Now bounce!"

"Elite, this is Haneef, and your friend Naja called the station when we announced that despite your mother playing us both out, you won the contest, front row seats to the concert and a chance to be on stage with me!"

I tap my foot and look around at the sea of students going into the school, then I look at Naja, who is standing here grinnin' and mush her dead in the head. "Do I sound impressed? I know you don't think I'm going to believe that this is Haneef and you all cared so much about me, that you gon' track me down. For what? Puleeze, this is Terrance. And since you playing so many games, I'ma be sure to tell all your boys on the basketball team that you ain't never had no booty, punk ass!"

"This is the last time," a deep male voice said, "before we hang up—"

"Do you—but if this is really Haneef, then sing something."

Suddenly the phone turned in a personal serenade, *"If I don't have you baby, I'ma go crazy . . . I need you in my life."*

At that moment, I knew that this was Haneef. "Jesus!" I screamed, right before I looked at Naja. She was jumping up and down.

"This is Haneef!" I screamed at the top of my lungs.

"Yes," he said. "You won the contest, and you have your friend Naja to thank! So do you want the tickets? They're two, so you can bring a friend."

"Boy," I said seriously. "Don't play with me."

"Come to the station," the DJ said, "by Saturday and pick them up."

Naja and I hugged tightly as we jumped up and down.

"Elite!" the DJ screamed. "Tell us the best station in Jersey!"

"Hot 102! Where my baby daddy lives! Holl-laaaah!"